ELIXIR

Richard Michaels Stefanik

Published by
RMS Publications Company
9299 Tower Side Drive #435
Fairfax, VA 20031

Library of Congress Catalog Card Number:
Available from the Publisher.

ISBN 1-882373-08-1

Printed in the United States of America

DEDICATED

to

K. C. CRAIG

whose

unconditional love

enabled me to write

Elixir

1

London during the Elizabethan Renaissance. A beautiful day: the sun blazes throughout the streets, around the corners, into the shops. White, magical light that shimmers off pieces of glass, blinds for a second, then speeds till it reaches a bed of flowers and bursts into the luminous spectrum of rainbow hues. People laughing, bustling about their business in a merry sort of way.

The Rose Playhouse. Inside, the theater is filled with a boisterous audience on holiday. Drink and food pass among the spectators while on stage Marlowe's "Doctor Faustus" is being performed. In the audience sit Michael and his guardian's wife, Jane Dee. Michael is an attractive, blond-haired young man of twenty-one. Twenty-one today, and this is his birthday gift from Jane. An afternoon at the theater, away from her husband's laboratory and library. Out into the daylight, the sunshine, on a warm summer day.

Jane is a modest woman in her mid-thirties. A virtuous, kind, gentle woman whose greatest concern in life is her duty to her husband, even if it means self-denial. Michael and Jane enjoy each other and have an understanding that doesn't need verbal expression.

The set on stage is decorated with a variety of astrological and magical paraphernalia, in an attempt to depict the study of Dr. Faustus. The astrological sign for the planet Mars, which represents the masculine principle, decorates a banner that hangs from ceiling to floor on the right side of the stage. On the left of the stage hangs a banner with the symbol for Venus, the feminine principle.

Michael and Jane are engrossed in the performance. Next to Michael sits a loud, loutish fellow with his lover at his side. They roar with laughter as they watch the performance. On stage are Faustus, Lucifer and Mephistopheles.

Lucifer: "Thou shouldst not think of God; think of the Devil."

Faustus: "Nor will I henceforth. Pardon me in this and Faust vows never to look to heaven, never to name God or pray to him, to burn his scriptures, slay his ministers, and make my spirit pull his churches down."

Lucifer: "Do so and we shall make it worth your while. Faustus, we have come from hell to show thee some pastime: sit down and thou shall see all the Seven Deadly Sins appear in their proper shapes."

The man next to Michael laughs, kisses his girlfriend, and takes a drink from his mug of liquor.

"Of the seven deadly sins, Lust is my favorite," he says as he laughs then kisses her again on the neck. While doing this, he accidently spills his drink on Michael's leg. Michael wipes himself off.

"I would have conjectured gluttony to be your favorite," says Michael to the lout.

"Eh, watch it lad, for Wrath is next in line." He looks Michael over quickly, then turns back to his lover. "I think Envy be his vice, or Sloth in the lack of effort to obtain a mate of his own." Back to Michael; "There on the stage you'll find a spouse. Choose Pride, for she has a lovely face, while the alternative, Greed, is far costlier than she's worth. But be sure to take the character to bed, and not the actor, lest you be in for an unpleasant..," winking at his lover, "or pleasant surprise."

"Ah, and you're the one to teach me the masculine role?" says Michael.

"But of course! Look on the stage. The signs are obvious. The male is ruled by Mars and made for war. The woman is made for love and ruled by Venus. They come together for pleasure and to give birth, then part to follow their own natures. All else is nonsense and sophistry. Watch, and listen to Faustus."

Faustus: "That sight will be pleasing to me as paradise was to Adam, the first day of his creation."

Lucifer: "Talk not of paradise nor creation, but mark this show; talk of the devil and nothing else. Come out."

Backstage, behind the curtains, stand the Seven Deadly Sins, costumed to express their specific vice. Gluttony, sloven and abrasive, walks to the front of the line.

7

"Out, Pride, begone. We have no need for you here, and Faustus waits to hear of your designs."

The other actors laugh as Pride walks onto the stage. Sloth walks up to Gluttony, takes him by the arm, and leads him back to his place in line.

"Stay in line, for you come after Envy and before Sloth, which is I. And we enter the stage one at a time."

Back on stage Lucifer continues with his lines, as Pride approaches them.

Lucifer: "Now, Faustus, examine them in their several names and dispositions."

Faustus: "What art thou, the first?"

Pride: "I am Pride, and I deny having any parents. I am like Ovid's flea: I can creep into every corner of a wench; sometimes like a periwig I sit upon her brow; next like a necklace I hang about her neck, or like a fane of feathers I kiss her lips; then turning myself into an embroidered undergarment, I do what I please. But fie, what scent is here. I'll not speak another word until the ground is perfumed and covered with Flemish tapestry."

The lout turns to Michael as Pride struts across the stage. "There's a comely lad for you, young man."

"Enough, you boor. Put your tongue back into your wench's mouth lest it be torn out and used as a sponge to soak up that swill."

He stands up and leans over Michael. "That I'd like to see you do, my lad."

"Sit down, sit down!" shout the spectators sitting behind him. The lout sits back in his seat. "After the show we'll settle this."

"Oh, leave the lad be," says his girlfriend. "Here, have another drink and attend to me."

He takes another drink, kisses her, then laughs. He sneers at Michael, then turns his attention back to the stage.

Faustus: "Thou art a proud Knave indeed. What art thou, the second?"

The actor playing Covetousness walks onto the stage.

Covet: "I am Covetousness, begotten of an old miser in an old leathern bag; and, might I have my wish, I would desire that this house and all in it were turned to gold, that I might lock you up in my chest. O my sweet gold."

Faustus: "What art thou, the third?"

Wrath: "I am Wrath. I had neither father nor mother; I leaped out of a lion's mouth when I was scarce half an hour old, and ever since I have run up and down the world with this case of rapiers, wounding myself when I had nobody to fight with. I was born in hell; and look to it, for some of you shall be my father."

Wrath then turns and walks to a corner of the stage.

Backstage, Gluttony pushes Envy forward.

"Quick, for this Faustus delivers his lines at a rapid pace. Methinks he desires to end this scene quickly for nature's release."

Envy walks onto the stage. Gluttony turns to Sloth and they both have a quiet snicker. But unbeknownst to them, from behind a set, a hooded figure walks towards them.

In the audience Jane whispers into Michael's ear.

"Are you enjoying yourself?" says Jane.

"Yes, yes, this is a fine gift," says Michael.

"For your twenty-first birthday. I'm sorry you have to sit next to that loudmouth."

"It's no problem. He's just drunk."

Faustus: "What art thou, the fourth?"

Envy: "I am Envy, begotten of a chimney sweeper and an oysterwife. I cannot read and therefore wish that all books were burned. I am lean with seeing others eat. O that there would come a famine through all the world, that all might die and I live alone; then thou shouldst see how fat I would be. But must thou sit while I stand? Come down, with a vengeance!"

Faustus: "Away, envious rascal!"

Envy turns and takes up his position next to Covetousness. Backstage, Gluttony still huddles with Sloth and Lust.

"Now it's my turn to strut upon the stage."

Gluttony turns and sees the hooded figure in front of him. The figure starts to walk onto the stage. Gluttony quickly grabs onto his arm.

"What is this? I come after Envy," says Gluttony as he holds onto the stranger's arm.

The stranger slowly turns and faces Gluttony, Sloth and Lust. Their eyes and mouths open wide in terror as they stagger away. Their horror is so great that they are unable to scream. They turn and run, tripping over each other in their efforts to escape from some unspeakable visage. The stranger then turns and walks out onto the stage.

The drunk next to Michael stares at the hooded figure as he walks across the stage. He turns to Michael.

"Who is this who comes in place of Gluttony?"

Faustus: "What art thou, the fifth?"

The stranger stands before Faust. He slowly pulls down his hood. He is extremely handsome, with smooth, well-structured features that display both intelligence and power. He smiles upon Faustus.

"My name is Monde, father of all strife. I come on warm afternoons when all seems right, when innocence and complacency know no plight. I'm the unexpected that puts hope to flight, and even awesome Wrath fears my might. My name is Monde, the Despair that changes day into night."

Monde lifts his arms up to the sky as thunderbolts light up the heavens. The winds howl and dark storm clouds blow up from the horizon. Faustus steps away from him. Monde smiles as he stares at Faustus, then the theater audience. His face begins to transform as his handsome features change into a horrible visage. Maggots and worms sprout from his head and face as a cynical leer spreads across his lips. Monde then slowly begins to levitate above the stage. Faustus, Lucifer and the other actors run from the stage. The crowd screams in terror as the audience quickly exits from the theater. Torrents of rain pour down upon them as the sky blackens. Monde continues to levitate. He laughs at the chaos he has created.

The drunk next to Michael screams in terror as he runs out of the theater, leaving his playmate to fend for herself. Michael and Jane stand still amid the turmoil. Jane turns her face away from Monde. Michael covers her with his cloak, to protect her from the rain. Michael stares at Monde's face. Their eyes meet and are locked together in a recognition of fate: in remembrance of things that happened long before birth, before reason, before hope. Michael turns away in disgust, then leads Jane out of the turmoil. Monde stares after them with hatred in his eyes, then pulls his cloak across his face, and vanishes into the darkness to which he had given birth.

Before they walk through the theater exit, Michael and Jane turn around and look to the stage. They watch

Monde as he dematerializes. As he slowly vanishes, he draws all the darkness back into himself and the sun again appears in the sky. They turn to leave, but suddenly Michael hears the voice of Monde call out his name. Michael looks to the stage, but there is no one there to be seen.

2

John Dee, magician, alchemist and astrologer to the Queen, is now in his mid-fifties. He wears black robes and scholar's cap, which contrast sharply with the long white beard that flows from his chin. Beside him stands Poohfer, his lab assistant, an unkempt, lanky man in his mid-thirties. In the middle of the room stands a furnace which they use for their alchemy experiments. The lab is decorated with alchemical paraphernalia, plants of an exotic nature, and astrological charts. Doctor Dee and Poohfer are preparing chemicals that are to be placed in the furnace.

"Be sure to do it right this time," snaps the irritable Dee.

Dee turns away from Poohfer and walks towards his desk. Poohfer glares at Dee's back with resentment, then mumbles under his breath.

"Then learn not to mumble, you babbling old fool."

Upon hearing this Dee stops short in his tracks, slowly turns, then sternly stares at Poohfer.

"Mind you. Your waste of my chemicals has cost me dearly already, Poohfer. And have some respect!"

Dee then sits down at his desk as Poohfer walks to the furnace.

Poohfer, again under his breath, "I only respect those that have respect for me!"

Poohfer carelessly throws a ladle onto the counter. Then with anger and frustration he starts to mix the chemicals, showing little care for what he is doing as he works.

Dee is reading through some documents on his desk when the bell by the door makes a tinkling sound. The door opens and in walks Edward Kelly, a handsome man in his mid-thirties. He stands tall, though he is really short in stature and in truth, a complete reprobate at heart.

"Morning Dee."

Dee looks up from his papers, sees that it's Kelly, then quickly turns back to his work.

"Ah, lawyer Kelly, I'm not yet ready with your chart."

Kelly cautiously peers about the room to make sure that they are alone. He sees Poohfer by the furnace.

"Morning, Poohfer."

Poohfer glances at Kelly with contempt, burps, then grunts a hello. He continues to work with the chemicals and grumble under his breath as a cat walks near his feet. Poohfer almost trips over the cat.

"Damn you, Cat!"

He kicks out at it but misses as the cat quickly

scurries under the workbench. Kelly watches the scene with amusement, then quickly pulls a chair up to the table and sits down next to Dee. Kelly then takes some papers from his pocket and puts them in front of Dee.

"John, I want your opinion on the quality of these signatures."

Dee stares at the two papers.

"What is this, Edward? Both documents have the same signature on them."

"Can you discern any difference?"

"No, none whatsoever."

Kelly is overjoyed. "Perfect! Now what do you think of this?"

Kelly takes a banknote from his pocket and gives it to Dee, who then studies it very closely. After a few moments he gives the note back to Kelly.

"It's a banknote. But, Edward, why do you show me these...?"

Dee then notices wet ink on his fingertips and a smudge on the banknote. Kelly laughs and quickly puts it back into his purse. Dee becomes outraged.

"Why do you bring such things to me? I have no interest in forgery!"

"John, John, patience, please."

"I'm an honest man! Don't involve me in any of your schemes."

"It's just a test, Dee, that's all. I needed a man with your abilities for a test of my skills. I won't bother you with this again."

"Beware of your ears, Kelly, least they be removed for forgery."

Kelly grabs hold of his ears in mock fright, then feigns righteous indignation as he speaks.

"John, this...this is just a hobby and a challenging exercise. I'd never really do it."

Dee stares at Kelly with disbelief. Kelly, realizing his statements are not being accepted, sighs with disappointment as he shrugs his shoulders.

Suddenly the door bursts open as Michael and Jane enter the room. Jane runs over to Dee and throws herself into his arms. Kelly's eyes light up when he sees Jane.

"Oh, John, John, it was horrible, just horrible!"

"What? What happened?" John says with concern.

"A demon, a horrible demon appeared at the theater."

"What demon? Where?"

"At the Rose," responds Michael. "In the middle of Marlowe's 'Faustus' a demon appeared on the stage."

"I've seen that often. It's in the script," laughs Kelly.

"Not this one," cries Jane. "Even the actors ran in fright, and the theater emptied in a minute. The sky became dark as rain poured from the thunder clouds," says the exasperated Jane.

"Perhaps it was a new version of the play," says Dee.

"No, this was no human performance, for the demon rose ten feet off the stage, and no dramatist can make the rain pour out onto the streets," replies Michael. "Here, feel our clothes. At one moment dry sunshine, the next wet night."

"A sudden storm. It happens all the time," replies Dee.

"And wires have been known to lift angels to heaven, so why not use them to lower demons to hell? Illusions. Tricks of the stage trade," responds Kelly.

Jane and Michael stare at each other in hopelessness, knowing that they will not be believed.

"We were there! This demon was no playwright's conceit," says Michael.

Kelly leans back in his chair and continues to admire Jane as she huddles in Dee's lap.

"John, you haven't introduced me. Who might these two be?" asks Kelly.

"I thought you already knew my wife Jane."

"If I knew her before you, I think she would not be yours, and I surely wouldn't have forgotten her name. I'm Edward Kelly. It's a pleasure."

"Surely, sir, you're much too bold," says Jane with reserve as she draws closer to Dee.

"Mind him not, 'tis but his way. And this is my ward Michael."

Michael holds his hand out to Kelly. "Good day, sir."

"And to you, sir," replies Kelly.

Dee attempts to calm Jane. "And this demon, did he give a name?"

"Monde," replies Michael. "He said his name was Monde as he wreaked havoc, then disappeared."

"Monde?" Dee whispers the name with concern.

"Do you know of him?" asks Michael.

"It's been many years since I heard his name. Did he see you? Speak to you?"

"I thought I heard him call my name," whispers Michael.

"A ruined birthday," says Jane sadly.

"Today?" asks Dee.

"Yes, did you forget? Twenty-one today," answers Jane.

Dee gets up from the table as worry begins to come over his face. "I'll have to think on this."

Suddenly Poohfer drops a metal canister. It makes a loud clattering sound as it crashes to the floor. The noise startles everyone.

Dee snaps at him with agitation in his voice. "Poohfer! Damn the man."

As Michael bends down to pick up the canister, a golden amulet falls out from inside his shirt and dangles from a chain around his neck. The light from the furnace flames makes it glitter. Kelly stares at the amulet with greed in his eyes.

Suddenly there is a minor explosion from the furnace. A billow of black smoke fills the room. This forces everyone to cough and get up from their chairs.

"Poohfer," screams Dee.

Kelly, Michael and Jane start for the door as Dee grabs Poohfer by the scruff of the neck and kicks him in the seat of the pants.

"Damn you, Poohfer. Clean up this mess before I return."

Dee walks out, leaving Poohfer alone in the smoke-filled room. Downcast and disgruntled, he mopes towards the furnace. The cat stares at Poohfer in a way that expresses his contempt for the man's stupidity. Poohfer growls, then kicks the cat, who screeches out in pain as it runs for cover.

3

Michael, Kelly and Jane stand by the doorway as Dee exits his lab. Dee takes out a piece of paper, writes some words on it, then hands it to Michael.

"Get me a new supply of these chemicals."

"Yes, sir."

"Jane and I will be at the house until this mess is cleaned up."

Dee and Jane then walk away. As Michael turns to go, Kelly takes him by the arm.

"Mind if I walk with you?" asks Kelly.

"No, not at all," replies Michael.

As they walk together down the street, Kelly continues to admire Michael's amulet.

"Interesting piece. Where was it purchased?"

"I didn't buy it. I've had it all my life."

"Would you be interested in selling it? I'd pay you with...gold coin."

"No, I could never do that. It's all I have left of my family."

They stop at a street corner as a horse-drawn carriage passes by. Across from them stands an elegantly dressed gentleman and next to him two extravagantly dressed beautiful women. Kelly becomes engrossed in the group and gazes at them with awe and admiration. He then glances down at his own ragged clothes and becomes embarrassed. The cuff of his shirt is ripped. He surreptitiously tries to tuck it under the sleeve of his jacket so that it will be hidden from sight. But the jacket sleeve is too short. Kelly then squeezes his shoulder to his neck in an attempt to make the sleeve longer. This works, and he is able to cover his ragged cuff with his jacket sleeve by tightly holding the sleeve against the palm of his hand with three of his fingers. Kelly glares at the gentleman with envy.

"Look how they admire him. One day I'll too have fine clothes and share the company of royalty."

"But not today," says Michael.

The two women leave the gentleman and walk towards Kelly. He becomes excited.

"Look, they're coming this way."

Kelly tightens the grip on his sleeve. When they are only a few feet away from him, he bows.

"Good day, ladies."

But his deep bow causes his elbow to tear through the sleeve. The women laugh at him before they continue on. Kelly is embarrassed.

"One day..."

"But as I said, not today."

"It's all appearance, that's all that is important. How you look, how you dress. It takes only a fine set of clothes for a man to be a king."

"Perhaps, but I think there is also the question of substance. Clothes can easily be bought with money."

"There you go, that's it. Gold. Gold is the substance on which all else rests. And the way to love is gold."

Kelly and Michael watch the two women as they walk away down the street. A funeral procession rounds the corner and advances up the street towards them. A coffin is carried on the shoulders of several pall-bearers. They are led by priests, and followed by a group of mourners. Michael becomes uncomfortable and turns away from the sight. Kelly notices this and smiles.

"What, does death bother you?" asks Kelly.

"No, no, I..."

"Get used to it, for you'll see many more like this before it's your turn to be carried out."

Kelly grabs him by the shoulders and spins him around.

"See what life's about and learn to laugh at its finale."

The priests walk past them. Kelly laughs and points

at their caps, which cover their ears and are tied tightly with string under their chins.

"I'd never be caught dead wearing caps as ridiculous-looking as that," says Kelly.

Michael then notices Suzanne, a beautiful young woman walking along with the procession. While the others are singing hymns with their eyes respectfully lowered to the ground, Suzanne watches the spectators along the side of the street as she silently walks. Michael gazes at her with fascination. Finally their eyes meet. Then, after a few moments Suzanne turns her eyes away, and instead looks down into her bouquet of flowers. She walks past Michael as he continues to gaze at her. After she walks a few more steps, she turns and glances back at him. Again he catches her eye. Embarrassed by the fact that he sees her interest, she stumbles and falls to the ground.

Michael runs to her assistance. He takes her hands and helps her up. They gaze at each other for a few moments. Michael then bends down to pick up her bouquet. At the same moment Suzanne also bends down. Their heads knock into each other and they both fall to the ground. As Suzanne falls a locket breaks from her neck. Neither Michael nor Suzanne notice this, but Kelly does. He quickly places his foot over the locket to hide it from view.

Michael and Suzanne stare at each other in a daze as they both sit on the ground. Suzanne's aunt, a matronly woman in her early forties, walks up to them.

"Come, Suzanne, thank the young man and let's be on our way."

"Thank you," Suzanne says to Michael.

She is then lead away by her aunt as Michael continues to gaze after her.

"Suzanne," Michael softly says to himself as he speaks her name.

"A pretty lass," says Kelly.

As the funeral procession continues on, Kelly lifts his foot and picks up the locket. Michael watches him as Kelly quickly places it into his pocket.

"What's that?" asks Michael.

"Oh, nothing, nothing."

"Then let me see."

"No, really, it's nothing."

"But then I insist, for I've always wanted to see what nothing looked like."

Kelly reluctantly takes the locket from his pocket and shows it to Michael. It has Suzanne's name imprinted on it. Michael stares at Kelly with disapproval, then takes the locket from him.

"I'll return it to the young woman," says Michael.

"I was afraid you'd do something like that."

"Good day, Mr. Kelly."

4

Kelly walks up to the door of his office, takes out a key, and opens the lock. Above the door hangs a sign which states "LAWYER." He enters the office and closes the door behind him.

He takes off his jacket, places it on a coat rack, then sits down at his desk. He takes the counterfeit banknotes from his pocket, holds them up against the light to inspect them once again, then smiles with satisfaction. He pulls the good money out of his wallet, stores it in a box on his desk, then places the counterfeit money back into the wallet. He next takes out the forged documents and re-examines them. The bell above his office door rings as a customer enters the room. Kelly quickly gathers up the papers and places them inside his desk. The customer is an overweight, jolly-looking fellow in his mid-forties.

"Hello, and how can I help you sir?"

The customer laughs nervously as he looks around the room to insure that they are alone.

"I hope that you can help me, sir. Yes, I truly hope so."

He winks at Kelly, then once again looks around the room. Kelly thinks the man's behavior to be a bit queer and begins to look around the room himself to see if there is anyone else about. Kelly then stands up and looks over the front of his desk to make sure no one is hiding there. Finally, he sits down.

"I can assure you that I can help, if you'd...just...tell me what it is..that you'd like."

The customer leans over the desk and whispers into Kelly's ear.

"There is a will that I'd like to have modified."

Kelly sits back in his chair and smiles at the man.

"But that would be simple. I'm highly qualified to make legal changes. Let me see the will."

The customer becomes downcast as he takes the will from his pocket and hands it to Kelly.

"There is one minor problem."

"And what might that be?"

"It's not my will."

The customer gulps as Kelly stares at him with disbelief. Kelly then smiles with mild interest as he leans forward.

"Well, then, whose will is it?"

"My uncle's."

"That's no problem. Just bring your uncle with you to my office."

The customer shakes his head with embarrassment. "I can't do that."

"And why not?"

He whispers into Kelly's ear. "He's dead."

Kelly begins to giggle, as does the customer. Their giggles then turn into laughter, as Kelly rubs his hands together in glee.

"Recently dead?" asks Kelly.

"Like this afternoon, dead."

"And I suppose the will is in need of 'minor' alterations?"

"Not exactly. The alterations have already been made in the document. What it needs now is a signature."

Kelly sits quietly and doesn't respond. The customer becomes nervous.

"One's skills will be rewarded with a handsome price."

"How attractive?"

"Ten gold coins."

"Such skill are in limited supply," responds Kelly.

"Fifteen?"

"Twenty."

"Twenty! But that's outrageous."

"Twenty gold coins will buy you not only an estate, but my eternal silence."

"Then, so be it," says the customer sadly.

Kelly smiles happily.

"Let me have it," says Kelly.

The customer then counts out twenty gold pieces and places them on the table. Kelly picks them up and drops them into his purse. The man then hands Kelly a piece of paper which contains the signature that he wishes to have copied.

"Here's a copy of the signature."

Kelly studies the signature, then meticulously begins to copy it as the customer closely watches over his shoulder. The forgery takes but a few moments. Kelly smiles with satisfaction as he holds up the forged document for the customer's inspection. The customer nods approvingly, then quickly snaps handcuffs on Kelly's wrists. Kelly is shocked.

"What means this, sir?"

The customer takes a badge out of his pocket and shows it to Kelly. "Not sir to you, but constable."

The constable then grabs Kelly by the scruff of the neck and drags him out the door.

"And be sure that in this case justice will be swift," says the constable.

5

John Dee and Jane are sitting at the table having their supper as Michael enters. He is carrying a package of chemicals in his arms and places them down on a table by the wall.

"Sit down," says Dee. "Have something to eat."

As Michael sits down, Jane gets up. She goes to the stove then returns with a plate of food for Michael.

"Have you finished reading that alchemy text?" asks Dee.

"No, not yet," replies Michael.

"And why not?"

"To be honest with you, sir, I find it to be boring."

"Boring? Of all people to find this boring!"

"Why do you expect this material to come easy to me?"

In exasperation Dee puts his head in his hands.

"The Elixir, Michael, the essence of nature, the basic substance that gives life, that doesn't interest you? That's not worth putting in time and effort to pursue?"

"The boy's tired," says Jane. "Let him rest."

"I'm almost three times his age, yet I continue!" Dee throws down his napkin, then gets up from the table. "I must return to the lab."

"Stay with us for a while longer. Sit at the table and talk," says Jane.

"And speak of what?"

"That doesn't matter," says Jane.

"It matters, it matters," says Dee. "You're but half my age. Then understand that what time I have left matters to me twice as much to me as your time does to you. And my quantity does not remain constant, but diminishes more and more as we stand."

Jane sadly turns away. Dee starts for the door, but then hesitates. He looks back at Jane, becomes sorry for his outburst, goes to her and puts his hand on her shoulder.

"I'm sorry, Jane. I'll try to return early." He kisses her on the forehead, then exits the room. Michael eats his food as Jane silently sits by the table.

"You're not happy," says Michael.

"No, that's not true. It's just his way."

"I wish he'd slow down and not drive himself and others so hard."

"He's a man with dreams."

"Yet in his dreams he forgets his wife."

"Hush, quiet. It's my duty to bear such things."

"Why?"

"Why? Because I'm his wife, and more than that, because I love him. And when you love someone, you give them all of your devotion."

"But then where be the devotion to Jane from Dee?"

"His needs are greater than my desires."

"Perhaps one day you'll think about your own needs."

Jane laughs and pats Michael on the hand. But I have you to do that. So tell me, how was your day?"

"I met a girl today."

"Oh, did you now? Tell me about her."

"She's beautiful and has blond hair. Her name is Suzanne. We met on Church Street."

"And what did you talk about?"

"Nothing, now that I think about it. Nothing at all. Except she did say, 'Thank you'."

"Such intimacy on a first meeting."

"She fell down to the ground twice, and I but once."

"Often it has been said that the male is the stronger of the species. Herein lies the proof."

Together they laugh as they enjoy their parlance.

"But I don't know where she lives."

"Suzanne? If it's the girl I think it is, she's staying on the edge of town, at the Albertson's."

"You know her?"

"Yes, we met a few days ago."

"And you didn't tell me?"

"I didn't think you'd be interested."

"Jane, you and Dee have been family to me, all the family I've ever known." Michael holds the amulet in his hand as he speaks. "I never knew my real father, and Dee never speaks about him. A woodsman, he says. A simple man. One can't know the dead and it's folly to seek that which can never be found. I have never even had a brother to share things with. I would have liked that. But something very special happened today, and this woman, that today I did see, this golden-haired Suzanne, I think, lies within my destiny."

Jane holds both his hands within her own and smiles at Michael. He takes Suzanne's locket from his pocket.

"She dropped this."

"A good cause for rendezvous."

"I'll return it in the morning."

"And what's wrong with tonight?"

6

Kelly is being pushed through the courthouse hallway towards the exit by the constable, who is now wearing a policeman's uniform. There are bandages on Kelly's head with blood stains on the spots where he used to have ears. He is whimpering as the constable pushes him along. The constable opens the front door. A crowd of people stand in the courthouse square. Kelly quickly slams the door shut.

"No, please, please have mercy," begs Kelly. "My reputation."

"Ha! Too late for that. Out!" says the constable in a self-righteous tone. He pushes Kelly out through the front door. The crowd turns and looks up at him. Everyone becomes silent. The constable bangs three times on the ground with his stick to get their attention.

"Hear ye, hear ye," bellows the constable. "This be Edward Kelly, convicted forger. Mark him well!"

The crowd points at Kelly's bandaged head and laughs as Kelly droops his head in humiliation. The constable pushes him down the stairs.

"Now get thee hence, and don't come back!"

Kelly wipes the tears from his eyes as he walks down

the courthouse stairs. The constable re-enters the court-house, slamming the doors of justice behind him. As Kelly walks through the crowd, people laugh and point at him. Little children gather around and throw sticks and stones at him. He runs down the street and is chased by the nasty little children and their mean, scraggly dogs.

7

Suzanne is walking down the hallway to her bedroom. As she passes her aunt and uncle's room she over-hears them talking about her.

She's a headstrong girl," says the aunt, "and won't take lightly to others deciding her life for her."

Suzanne stops by the door and listens more intently to their conversation.

"It's a good match," says the uncle. "A handsome young man from a fine family. And given that my brother left but small dowry for her, she'll do no bet-ter."

"I can but foresee one small problem."

"And what's that?"

"Suzanne has always detested William," says the aunt.

Upon hearing this name, Suzanne's eyes bulge as she mouths his name in utter amazement without uttering a sound. Her rage builds until finally she screams the name out at the top of her lungs as she barges into the bedroom.

"WILLIAM!!!!!!"

Her aunt and uncle are sitting in the bed with their nightgowns on. Both are startled by Suzanne's sudden appearance and intense rage.

"I'll not marry that sniveling snob," she screams at them.

Her uncle is outraged by her behavior. "What, listening at our door?" He stands on the bed with the sheet held up to his chin.

"And what are you doing bursting into our room?"

"Yet it's all right for you to rummage through my life," replies Suzanne.

"Show some respect, girl," answers the uncle. "You have neither the intelligence nor the experience to make decisions concerning your future. All you have is blind fury and a stubborn will."

Suzanne's rage boils over as she screams at the top of her lungs. "WHAT, ME?? BLIND FURY??" Then, in her intense rage, she kicks the nearest bedpost. It snaps in two and the canopy collapses on her aunt and uncle, completely covering up the two of them.

"It's my life and I'll live it as I choose!"

The uncle stands up and speaks while still covered by the canopy. "As long as you live in my house, you'll do as I say."

"Then I'll leave in the morning," screams Suzanne.

She storms to the door and slams it shut with such power that the room shakes and the doorknob comes off in her hand. Still in a rage, she walks down the hallway, enters her room, and slams that door shut. Finally there is silence, but only for a few moments. Her door reopens and through it is thrown the door-knob, which noisily bounces down the hallway floor. She then again shuts her door.

8

Michael, carrying Suzanne's locket in his hand, sings a sweet song to himself as he walks up a country path.

"All I want is a tender lass, of a meek and mild manner..."

Suddenly the still night air is broken by the wild shrieking scream of an enraged banshee. Michael grabs hold of his chest and stops dead in his tracks. The scream comes from the direction of the courtyard. He puts the locket into his pocket, then jumps up and clings to the top of the wall. He pulls himself up just in time to see Suzanne let out another scream of rage, with her fists clinched and held up against the sky.

Michael slowly slides down along the wall. When on the ground he shakes his head with confusion and disbelief. Once again he climbs to the top of the wall and looks across the courtyard. The full moon in the night sky casts enchanting, shadowy beams of light across the courtyard. The balcony is now empty. He looks around to insure that the courtyard is still empty, then jumps down to the ground. When he hits the dirt he twists his ankle and cries out in pain.

Suddenly he hears a noise from the balcony above. Michael quickly scrambles to hide among the bushes as Suzanne appears. She leans over the railing and looks down into the courtyard. Michael watches her from his hiding spot below. Not seeing anyone, Suzanne turns and begins to walk back into her room. Michael leans forward in order to get a better view of her. As he does this he puts pressure on his ankle which again forces him to cry out in pain as he collapses to the ground. Suzanne rushes back to the edge of the balcony.

"WHO'S DOWN THERE..." she yells, but her voice quickly trails off when she sees that it is Michael. She quickly tries to suppress her shrewishness and transform herself back into a very gentle, feminine creature. But the transition is far from smooth. Michael sits in the center of the courtyard as he lovingly gazes up at Suzanne.

"Suzanne," whispers Michael softly.

"Ah yes, the boy from the street."

Michael takes her locket from his pocket and lifts it up to her.

"You dropped this. I wanted to return it."

"Then you may bring it up."

Michael stands and wobbles towards the vines that are at the base of the balcony. He tries to climb up the vines, but instead falls back to the ground.

"Are you hurt?" asks Suzanne with concern.

"My ankle. I sprained it while jumping off the wall."

"Silly, why didn't you use the courtyard door?"

Suzanne points to an open door that leads into the courtyard. Michael looks at it, then feels stupid.

"Well, never mind," says Suzanne, "but next time..." She realizes what she is about to say and stops herself in mid-sentence. She steps away from the edge to be out of Michael's view and reprimands her forwardness by slapping herself on the wrist. Then, in a dignified manner, she returns to the edge of the balcony.

Suzanne sighs with disappointment at Michael sitting on the ground. She then looks around the courtyard to see if anyone else is watching. Assured that they are alone, she shrugs her shoulders, lifts her nightgown up above her knees, steps over the balcony railing, and begins to climb down the vines. When she reaches the ground, she walks over to Michael.

"Now let me see your leg," she says.

"Here, first take your locket."

He holds it out to her. She smiles at him as she takes it in her hand.

"This is the second time today I thank you, and I still don't know your name."

"Michael."

"Well then, hello, Michael. Now let me see that ankle." Suzanne begins to nurse the sprain. "Nothing appears to be broken."

She then puts her hand on his brow to see if he has a fever. Michael takes hold of her hand.

"It's not there that I feel the damage has been done."

"He then place her hand on his heart. Suzanne is surprised by his forwardness and at first tries to pull away, but Michael then pulls her on top of him and kisses her on the lips. The sudden sound of a metal door opening tears them apart.

"Suzanne!" calls out the aunt from a far corner of the courtyard.

Suzanne quickly helps Michael up to his feet and hides him behind some bushes. She then stands in front of them as her aunt walks into the courtyard.

"Suzanne, what are you doing out here?"

"Just getting some fresh air, auntie."

"Are you alone? I thought I heard other voices."

"Quite alone. I was thinking out loud about the present state of the world's respect for women. Mine was a solitary discourse."

"Suzanne, go to bed. We'll discuss this in the morning."

"Ah, to bed. The appropriate place for a creature like me."

"I hope that one day you'll respect the opinions of

those who love you," says the aunt sadly, "before any grave damage is done."

Suzanne's aunt then turns and leaves the courtyard. Suzanne helps Michael out from the bushes.

"You must go now," she says as she leads him to the side door.

"I want to talk to you some more," says Michael.

"No, I don't think so."

"Yes, I must," he says as he takes hold of her hand. "Now."

"No, I can't here."

"Then where?"

"In the orchard by the lake. Tonight. At midnight. The moon is full. There will be plenty of light. Tonight."

Suzanne hesitates, then agrees. Michael tries to kiss her again, but she gently pushes him away. She takes a scarf from her sleeve and gives it to him.

"Here, take this as a gift."

Michael takes the scarf, then turns and walks away as she closes the door behind him. Suzanne smiles and leans against the door as she basks in thoughts of romance.

9

Two priests are sitting on a park bench enjoying the cool night air. On the bench next to them lie their caps. Behind the bench is a clump of bushes. There is a slight, silent rustling in the bushes, and finally two hands appear which separate some of the branches.

Kelly pokes his bandaged head through the opening. He sees that the priests are engrossed in their conversation, so he slowly crawls up to the bench and steals one of their caps. He quickly crawls back into the bushes. Once there, he begins to unravel the bandages from his head.

10

Dee is working near the furnace as Jane enters the lab. She is wearing a white nightgown with a shawl wrapped around her shoulders, and carries a lighted candle in her hands. Dee is completely absorbed in his work and is unaware of her presence.

"John," she says softly.

Dee doesn't hear her as he peers into the bubbling liquid in the furnace. Jane moves closer and touches him on the arm. He then slowly turns and looks at her.

"Jane," he says absentmindedly.

He looks back at the furnace, mixes the chemicals, then turns back to Jane. He points at the chemicals brewing in the fire.

"Look, it's mixing as it should."

"Come to bed, John, it's late."

But he is still absorbed in his work. "No, you go now. I'll be up in a little while."

He smiles at Jane who nods her head in disbelief.

"I will, in a short while," he reaffirms. "You go ahead."

Dee turns back to the furnace and his work. Jane sighs,

then leaves the room. A little while later she enters their bedroom. Jane places the candle on the nightstand, removes her shawl, then gets into bed. She lies on her side and with her hand softly caresses the empty space by her side. Then, after a few moments, she turns over, blows out the candle, and settles down to sleep.

11

It is night, and an old woman is walking alone down a country road. She becomes startled as she sees a figure approaching her from the darkness. But then, with a moment of recognition, she relaxes, blesses herself, and devoutly bows to the man.

"Good evening, Reverend," she says.

The old woman kisses his hand and continues on her way. The man turns around to watch her go. It's Edward Kelly wearing the priest's cap. His expression changes from mild shock to amusement. He readjusts the cap over his ears, tightens the string around his neck, then proceeds down the road towards a tavern in the distance.

Inside the tavern, several peasants are sitting at tables as they eat their dinners. The innkeeper, a large, burly man, stands behind a counter reading an old manuscript. Next to him on the counter is a small sack that contains a red powdery substance. Some of this red powder lies on the counter. The innkeeper scratches his head in frustration, for he is having little success comprehending the book. The waiter walks up to him.

"Have you made sense of it yet?" asks the waiter.

"Nah, it's rubbish to me," says the innkeeper.

"Then the night would have been better spent in a warm bed than the cold graveyard," says the waiter as he walks away with disgust.

"I'll turn a profit on this yet," snarls the innkeeper.

The front door opens wide as Kelly enters the inn. He meanders through the people in the dining area as he makes his way towards the innkeeper. Ann, an attractive but virtuous-appearing, buxom young woman sits at one of the tables by herself. Kelly eyes her lustfully, but when she looks up at him he disguises his desire behind a visage of dignity. Ann respectfully smiles at him, and Kelly nods in acknowledgement. He then walks up to the innkeeper who is still trying to decipher the manuscript.

"Supper and a room for the night," says Kelly.

The innkeeper turns away to get him a room key. Kelly glances at the manuscript and sees that it contains alchemical symbols. He begins to flip through the pages with interest. The innkeeper notices Kelly's attraction to the book. He thinks for a moment, rubs his chin, then smiles.

"An old curiosity, sir," says the innkeeper.

"Are you a student of the lore?" asks Kelly.

The innkeeper nods. " And don't you think it's of some value?"

Kelly, realizing that a deal is beginning to take shape, downplays his interest.

"Only to a scholar like myself. It has historical value as an oddity of the intellect, but is of no material worth."

The waiter stands behind Kelly and winks to the innkeeper his approval of the sale to the sucker. The innkeeper then leans towards Kelly and whispers into his ear.

"By your attire, sir, I can tell that you're a man of the true faith," says the innkeeper. Kelly solemnly nods his head in agreement. "This manuscript and sack of red dust were once the possessions of a disbeliever, a heretic of the faith."

"No, can it be so?" says Kelly with feigned astonishment.

"It's the truth. I swear on it. And James here can bear witness to that," he says as he points to the waiter. The waiter solemnly nods his head in agreement.

"But then how did you get it?" asks Kelly.

The innkeeper becomes puzzled for a moment, but then arrives at what he feels to be an appropriate answer.

"Sir, being the good Christians that we are we decided that it would come to no good if the earth were polluted with the likes of this. So last night we released it from her cavity."

"Eh?" asks Kelly, not understanding the innkeeper's intent.

"We dug it out of his grave," says the waiter.

"Uh, how gruesome an affair," responds Kelly in feigned shock. "But pray tell, sirs, did he smile upon your labors?"

"That he did," replies the waiter, "until I removed the grin from his face."

The waiter places his hand into his pocket and pulls out four tarnished gold teeth that he had taken from the dead man's mouth. Both the waiter and the innkeeper begin to cackle in outrageous laughter, which finally affects Kelly as he fights a losing battle to suppress a smile. After they have all regained their composure, Kelly quickly grabs hold of the manuscript.

"Then this must be disposed of properly," says Kelly.

The innkeeper and waiter look at each other with concern, then the innkeeper grabs at the book. He and Kelly struggle over it until finally the waiter also joins in on the side of the innkeeper. Together they pull it away from Kelly. Everyone attempts to regain his composure and sense of dignity, while eyeing the manuscript carefully. The innkeeper clears his throat, then speaks in a serious tone.

"Methinks that there's much value contained within these pages and this crushed stone." He opens up the sack and reveals the reddish powder to Kelly. "It's believed that the heretic had the ability to turn base metal into gold."

Both the innkeeper and the waiter watch Kelly very

closely to see how he reacts to this statement, but he holds himself well. Kelly slowly lifts up the sack of crushed stone in one hand, then picks up the manuscript with the other. He moves his hands up and down as if they were trays of a scale as he weighs their value.

"Gentlemen, I'm prepared to compensate you for the weight of your labors," says Kelly. "Shall we say, three pounds."

The waiter stands behind Kelly and by moving his head upwards indicates that the innkeeper should demand more.

"I think ten pounds would be more fitting for the night's work of two men," responds the innkeeper.

The price is too high for Kelly. Once again he weighs the objects in his hands, then sets them down on the counter.

"No, this load can be but five pounds, and no more," he responds.

"I think not," says the innkeeper. "The world is large and there are many who would find this to be of worth."

"As you wish," says Kelly, "and to show that there are no hard feelings, I'll gladly advertise your possessions...and labors...among the clergy I meet in my travels."

The mouths of both the waiter and innkeeper drop to the floor. The waiter quickly indicates to the innkeeper that he should accept Kelly's offer.

"Uh, be not hasty sir. Your offer...is acceptable."

Kelly reaches into his pocket and takes out some gold coins. The waiter and innkeeper smile at each other with smug satisfaction, and out of the corner of his eye Kelly sees them mocking him. Kelly smiles at them, puts the coins back into his pocket, and takes out his wallet which contains the counterfeit banknotes. He takes out some banknotes and hands them to the innkeeper, who joyfully takes them. Kelly then picks up the manuscript, sack of powder, his room key, and turns to leave.

"Just a minute," says the innkeeper. Kelly freezes in his tracks. "You forgot to sign the register."

Kelly takes pen in hand and signs his name. The innkeeper reads the signature as Kelly departs.

"Goodnight, Reverend Kelly."

As Kelly climbs to the staircase to his room, Ann watches him from below.

12

Inside his room, Kelly sits on his bed as he tries to read through the manuscript. Like the innkeeper, he also is having difficulty understanding it.

"Perhaps Dee can decipher this," he says to himself.

Suddenly there is a knock on his door. Kelly places the book on a nightstand and goes to the door. He opens it and sees Ann standing in the doorway.

"Please, sir, a few moments of your time," she says.

Kelly opens the door wider as Ann enters his room. He then sticks his head out into the hallway to make sure she hasn't been followed. Satisfied, he goes back into the room and locks the door behind him. He sits on the edge of the bed as Ann stands in front of him.

"How can I help you, my child?"

"I need some comfort your holiness."

Kelly lustfully gazes over the luscious body of the woman. The tension within him caused by his attempts to maintain an external appearance of control causes him to slightly sway back and forth as his voice takes on a shrill pitch.

"What kind of comfort?" he asks.

Ann becomes worried, and slowly begins to back up towards the door. Kelly quickly clears his throat and tries to regain his composure.

"Excuse me please, my dear, a slight cold," he explains.

Ann relaxes, then pleasantly smiles at Kelly.

"Why is it you travel alone?"

"I'm off to visit my father in London."

"Ah, then your home's in the country?"

"Yes, my father's a widower, so I live with the nuns in a rural convent."

"Then you're familiar with the ways of the cloth."

"Very much so."

Ann opens the shawl that is wrapped around her shoulders. She thereby exposes more of her voluptuous form to Kelly's gaze. His eyes open wide while his head begins to involuntarily bob up and down as he looks over her body. He starts to whimper.

"I need your help, for lately I've become obsessed with desires of the flesh."

Ann falls to her knees as she clasps Kelly's legs He puts his hands on her shoulders as his whimpers increase. Ann also begins to cry. Then, as Ann presses her body more tightly against his knees, Kelly begins to lose control of himself.

54

"Please pray with me so I can control my lusts," pleads Ann.

Kelly kneels on the floor next to her and together they pray, shoulder to shoulder, with eyes closed. Kelly slowly opens one eye and lustfully gazes at Ann's heaving breasts. He takes her by the shoulders and lifts her up from the floor. He then holds her tightly against him.

"Have faith, have faith," moans Kelly.

Ann clings to him.

"Trust me, and may the Lord help us work out these passions," he whispers into Ann's ear.

"Yes, yes, I trust you."

Kelly then spins her around and tosses her onto the bed. He tears off his shirt and jumps on top of her. At first she protests, but then finally succumbs to his spiritual wisdom. They quickly tear off each other's clothes and fling them into the air as the they passionately toss about on the bed.

13

Dee stands in front of the furnace in his laboratory as he watches the flames cook the chemicals. He is very tired. He sits down in a chair, rubs his eyes, then gazes into the flames. The walls around him are lined with bookcases that are filled with dusty old manuscripts. Dee picks a book up from the side table and starts to read it, but after a few moments he drops the book to the floor.

"It's over," he says with resignation."I've wasted my life in futility. Enough. I give up." He sinks down into his chair, a tired, beaten man. "I can no longer continue. I will no longer continue," he says weakly. "I must not go on...I'll go on," he says to himself softly.

His eyes once again begin to flicker with life. He reaches down for the book on the floor, picks it up, then places it on his lap.

Suddenly a strange whirling sound fills the room. Flickers of moonlight come through the window. They reflect off the dust that floats up from the floor through the shaft light. These flickers then increase in intensity and grow to the size of snowflakes. The air begins to shimmer as a crystalline form takes shape, until it forms itself into the spirit of Samuel the Wizard. He is a huge man with a long blond hair and a full beard.

56

"The time has come," says the wizard.

"But I don't know if Michael is ready," responds Dee.

"He will be. He has to be."

"Monde...he said that Monde appeared to him today," whispers Dee with concern expressed in his voice.

"Then things will happen quickly," responds Samuel.

Then, out of the air in front of them, Samuel produces a crystal ball, which hovers in front of Dee.

"What is this?" asks Dee.

"A gift. Use it wisely, for it will give you access to other spirits who'll answer your questions. Take it."

Dee anxiously reaches out for the ball. He takes it into his hands, then gazes into the crystal. It's filled with a silvery mist and rainbow specks of light. Dee places the crystal on his table. He then turns back towards the window, but Samuel has disappeared. Dee is puzzled, but then looks back to the table where the crystal remains.

14

In a meadow near the lake stands a grove of apple trees. Suzanne sits on a branch in one of the trees as she picks apples and collects them into a pile on her lap. A full moon lights the cloudless sky. Michael approaches from the distance. Suzanne is excited to see him, but hides herself among the branches.

As Michael walks near the tree, Suzanne drops an apple near his feet. Preoccupied with his thoughts, Michael doesn't notice the apple. This infuriates Suzanne, who then takes an apple from her lap and throws it at him. The apple hits Michael in the back of the head and knocks him to the ground. Suzanne becomes worried, fearing that she may have hurt him, but she relaxes when he gets up. He rubs the back of his head as he looks around while Suzanne nonchalantly continues to pick apples. Michael finally notices her and holds up the apple.

"Is this yours?"

Suzanne reacts as if nothing has happened and that she is seeing him for the first time.

"Oh Michael, are you here already? What's that you have? An apple?" She acts disappointed. "Oh, and I was going to offer you one."

Suddenly, the branch on which she is sitting begins to
58

crack. Her eyes open wide with fright as she grabs onto it. The apples fall from her lap and bombard Michael. The branch cracks some more and lowers her precariously further towards the ground. Finally it breaks completely and Suzanne begins to fall. Michael, of course, catches her in his arms. She puts her arm around his neck and smiles at him as he holds her. He attempts to kiss her but she sharply rebuffs him. She becomes coy.

"You may put me down now," she says.

Michael doesn't follow her command but instead continues to hold her. She playfully struggles to get out of his arms, and puts one leg to the ground while he still holds her about the waist. Finally she frees herself from him and arranges her clothes back in order. She starts to walk towards the lake. Michael follows her.

"Last night I thought I heard a banshee screaming in your courtyard." Suzanne cringes. "That is," continues Michael, "before we spoke."

Suzanne is embarrassed. "I was upset before we met."

"About what?"

"My aunt and uncle trying to run my life."

"Parents have a tendency to do that, and they always justify it by appealing to a notion of responsibility."

"In any case, I've resolved the issue. I've decide to run away."

"What's this?"

"It's true, and I have a plan. Since I was a child I always believed that it was my destiny to one day marry a great wizard."

"There are no such beings. You best settle for a man."

"No, that's not true. I didn't grow up here, in England, but in the mountains of Bohemia. Once a great wizard lived in that land. He could heal the sick and make barren women fertile. Legend says that he had a son, and that one day this son would return. It's my dream to marry that wizard's son."

"An old wives' tale."

"No, for I've seen his mother's grave and the ruins of his father's house."

"And how will you know when you find him?"

"By the strength and powers that he'll possess."

"Stay here with me, Suzanne. I've just found you and now you want to leave."

She takes his hand. "Be happy for me, Michael. This is my life's dream. And think on this. I hope he'll be as handsome and gentle as you."

"It's a long journey, and I fear you'll find much sadness if you take that road."

"Don't worry, I'm the equal of any man."

60

"Perhaps in spirit, and before the laws of the city. But on the highway only brute force reigns, and therein will your weaknesses be shown."

"How so, are we not both of the same species?"

"There's much reason to doubt that," he says with a smile.

Suzanne becomes angry. "Oh really. Then we must quickly part if you refuse to wish me a happy farewell."

Suzanne starts to walk away. Michael runs after her and takes her by the arm.

"So there's no hope for my cause."

"All I can give you is the moment, for I leave at dawn."

They have reached the edge of the lake. Suzanne bends down and touches the water with her hand. She then stands up. The moon is full at their backs as it seems to fill the night sky. As they stand together at the edge of the lake, their images, equal in length to their heights, reflect on the surface of the water, along with the image of the moon at their backs.

"The water is warm, swim with me."

"Why don't I leave with you in the morning?"

"No, that journey I'll make alone, but tonight you can come with me."

She quickly removes her clothes and dives into the

water. Michael does the same and dives in after her. He still wears the amulet around his neck. Suzanne starts to swim across the lake as Michael swims after her. He finally catches her in the middle of the lake. They wrap their arms around one another and kiss. Their entwined bodies slowly sink under the surface of the water. Bubbles swirl about them as they continue to kiss and embrace under the water. Finally, after what seems like an eternity, they surface. Suzanne laughs as she again begins to swim away. Michael follows her. When she reaches the shore, she climbs out of the water. She begins to run through the meadow with Michael following after her. Finally he catches her and pulls her to the ground. Suzanne notices the amulet and takes it in her hand.

"What's this?"

"A gift from my father."

He takes it from his neck and holds it out to her.

"It was meant to protect and bring me love. I want you to have it." He then places it around her neck. They kiss, then make love.

15

Michael is still sleeping on the grass while Suzanne finishes dressing. It's still night. She takes the amulet in her hand and gazes at it as it shimmers in the moonlight. She then places it beneath her blouse, kneels down next to Michael, and kisses him on the forehead. "In your dreams, remember me," she whispers, then she stands and walks away as Michael begins to stir in his sleep.

Michael dreams that he is walking through a dark wood towards a clearing. He hears voices chanting in the distance. He slowly creeps through the underbrush towards the sound of the voices. He separates some branches and sees a large bull standing in the center of the clearing. Next to the bull is a beautiful woman dressed in white. She rests her hand on the bull's neck. They are at ease with one another.

Into the clearing walk several men dressed in ceremonial white robes. They utter unintelligible prayers to the bull. All the men in unison lift their hands up to the night sky, towards the star Sirius. They then move their hands towards the eastern horizon where the constellation Virgo is rising. Michael is hypnotized by the ceremony.

Suddenly, from behind him, he hears a twig snap. He quickly turns around. Behind him stand two naked men who are completely painted over in the color blue. They seize Michael and drag him into the clearing. They take him to the edge of a pit which is at least ten feet deep. They then push him into the pit.

The chants of the men become louder. Logs are rolled across the top of the pit, thereby making a grid above Michael. The men lead the bull to the edge of the grid. They then quickly take out their swords and slaughter the bull. It falls dead on the grid. The bull's blood falls onto Michael. He raises his arms to protect himself. He then opens his mouth to scream in horror, but no sound comes out.

The dream continues. Michael is now running through the woods. He is still drenched red with the bull's blood. He looks behind him to see if he is followed. When he turns forward again he runs into a post. The collision knocks him off his feet. From the foot of the post he looks up. It is a cross, and nailed to the cross is a ram, whose blood flows down to the ground.

In terror, Michael quickly stands up and again starts to run. Finally he comes to the edge of a stream. Two fish flounder on the grass by the bank. Michael picks them up and gently places them back into the stream. They swim away with the current.

Michael looks up to see a tall man standing over him. The man carries a large urn that is filled with water. He pours the water over Michael, which washes away all the blood. Water flows over Michael's head and into his eyes. This temporarily blinds him. Michael rubs his eyes with his hands. When he reopens them he gazes at the reflection of himself in the stream. The water bearer is gone. Michael stands up. He is completely dry, clean, and dressed in green garments from head to foot.

Michael awakes at the spot in the meadow where Suzanne had left him. He is still naked. He looks around and sees that Suzanne is gone. At his feet lie his clothes, which Suzanne had gathered for him before she left. He looks at the night sky. It's filled with bright, shining stars. A comet flashes across the sky.

Michael then looks across the meadow. In front of him stands a large oak tree. The tree begins to make a loud humming sound. After a few moments the image of Samuel appears in the midst of the tree. He holds his arms out to Michael. Michael becomes frightened and steps back. In the hands of Samuel appear a crystalline glass vessel filled with some shimmering liquid substance. The Elixir.

Michael stares at the scene in complete amazement. Again, he rubs his eyes. But when he opens them and looks at the tree, the image of Samuel and the Elixir remain. Slowly, the intensity of the humming decreases and the images disappear from the tree as the tail of the comet evaporates against the star filled black sky.

In complete silence Michael stands alone in the night.

16

Poohfer and Dee stand near the table. In the center of the table sits the crystal ball.

"Yes, I said a spirit!" says Dee with annoyance. "Last night, here, in this very room."

Poohfer eyes Dee with disbelief. Dee senses his skepticism.

"You don't believe me, do you?" says Dee.

Poohfer then clears his throat and tries to be accommodating.

"Um, was it a large spirit or a small spirit?" asks Poohfer.

Dee realizes that he's being pampered and becomes enraged.

"Large or small? I'll show you large or small. Where's my swatting stick?"

Dee starts to search the room for his swatting stick as Poohfer backs away.

"Poohfer, where's my swatting stick?"

Just then Kelly enters the room. Though his clothes

are disheveled, he still wears the priest's cap. He carries the manuscript and sack under his right arm. Poohfer stares at Kelly with dismay. He then quickly makes the sign of the cross and starts to walk out of the lab.

"Poohfer, where are you going?" shouts Dee.

Poohfer shakes his with anxiety. "Two conversions in one day...'tis more than mere coincidence. Surely Doomsday's near and I've got confessions to make." He quickly runs out of the lab.

Dee looks at Kelly's cap. "What's that on your head?"

"Ah, it's a sad tale to tell of betrayal, deception, injustice and..."

"And surely larceny played a major role."

"No, I think it were but a minor part," says Kelly as he sighs deeply. "But never mind that. It's done with. This is what I want to show you."

Kelly hands the alchemy manuscript to Dee.

"I purchased it last night at a rural inn. It's rumored that the original owner used it and this red powder to turn metal into gold. But for the life of me I can't decipher a word of it."

Dee quickly skims through the pages and becomes absorbed in the book.

"Possibly," says Dee. "One thing is certain, these are not trivial thoughts. Have you tested the powder yet?"

"I haven't had the chance."

"Then quick, to the furnace."

Dee becomes excited as he picks up a piece of lead from the workbench. He places this into a metal pot, then puts the pot into the furnace. Next he pours some of the red powder onto a sheet of paper.

"May these specks of stone be the product of a philosopher's wisdom," Dee prays as he folds the paper. The flames flicker around the pot as the piece of lead begins to melt. Dee then tosses the paper that contains the powder into the melting lead. Kelly and Dee peer into the flames as they watch the paper burn within the boiling lead. After a few moments they jump back in amazement, for the lead has turned to gold. Dee quickly takes the pot from the furnace and pours the molten gold into a mold.

"Jane, Jane," calls out Dee. "Damn, she should be here to see this, to see that I've not been wasting my time. A most auspicious day. First the crystal last night, now this. It seems that finally my years of toil will no longer be rewarded with futility and barren results."

Kelly's face is filled with greed as he stares at the gold. Kelly grasps the sack of powder with a sense of victory.

"Gold! And this be my source."

"I must have some," says Dee, "to analyze its components and get to the Elixir which lies at its core."

"And of what value is this Elixir? Can it make more gold?"

"No, but it's the very essence of life itself."

"Then I have no need of it, for the pump in my chest suffices to drive me forward. But I'll give you a small portion for your pleasure."

Dee holds out a piece of paper. Kelly taps a few specks of the powder from the sack onto the sheet. But only a few specks. Dee looks at him with disappointment.

"There's not much powder here," says Kelly in an attempt to justify his selfishness.

"That's why we must study it and learn to make more," answers Dee.

"Oh," replies Kelly, as he taps over a few more specks. "Will that be enough?"

Suddenly the door opens and Michael walks into the lab. Kelly quickly throws a piece of cloth over the gold. Michael appears to be confused and has a bewildered expression on his face. Behind him enters Jane.

"What's wrong?" asks Dee.

"Everything," replies Michael. "Last night I lost my love and I think also my mind."

"What do you mean, lost your mind?" asks Dee.

"In the meadow I had dreams and visions."

"Visions of what?"

"An old man with a long beard appeared among the branches of an oak tree. He held his arms out to me and within his hands appeared a crystalline vessel that contained a shimmering liquid substance."

"Did the spirit speak to you?"

"No, but he beckoned me to come to him. What does this mean?"

Dee leans back in his chair and ponders on how best to answer this question. He rubs his beard for a few moments, then begins to speak.

"It's time to unveil the mystery. That was the spirit of your dead father, and within his hands he held the Elixir."

Michael becomes confused. "But you told me my father was a simple woodsman."

"I lied to protect you from those who may want to do you harm. Your father was a great wizard, and so, too, were you born to be."

"And this Elixir that he held in his hand?" asks Michael.

"It's to be your possession," replies Dee. "But first, sit down, and let me tell you the story of your birth." Michael sits down, along with Jane and Kelly, as Dee begins his tale.

Elixir

"This happened over twenty years ago, yet I remember it vividly. Your father's name was Samuel, and he lived in the mountainous regions of Bohemia..."

* * *

Samuel is digging up plants while Dee, twenty years younger, watches him. Samuel carefully inspects each of the herbs before he places them into a sack. Dee appears to be impatient.

"Samuel, I'm not interested in herbal medicines. I've traveled all the way from England to speak of more important matters."

Samuel gets up and continue to walk through the forest in search of other plants. Dee follows after him.

"And what is this object that you seek knowledge of."

"The Elixir."

"Yet not that of the medicines of nature?"

"But it's the Elixir that is the essential source of all power. It is that which I desire to know."

"But not of nature's morning dew," replies Samuel.

Suddenly he hears the cries of a bird that is trapped within a bush. Samuel spreads apart the branches and reaches in for the bird. He holds it within his hands as he gently pets it. The bird's wing is broken. Samuel kneels on the ground and softly utters an incantation as he places the palm of his hand on the earth. A soft green energy radiates up from the ground and flows into his hand. Samuel then rubs this energy over the bird's wing. The wing heals. He then tosses the bird up in the air. Both Samuel and Dee watch it fly away. They then continue to walk on through the forest towards Samuel's hut, which lies in a clearing on the far side of a pond.

When they enter the hut, Samuel is greeted by his wife Martha. She is pregnant. Dee walks over to the fireplace, sits down in a chair, and immediately starts to read a book. Samuel playfully smiles at Martha, then approaches Dee. He puts his hand over the page that Dee is reading.

"I thought you said you wanted knowledge?" asks Samuel.

"That I do," replies Dee.

"Well, you won't find any knowledge you seek in there."

Samuel removes his hand. Dee looks down at the book and sees a lizard on the page. The little lizard sticks his tongue out at Dee. He shrieks with horror as he throws the book down to the floor. Martha comes over and holds onto Samuel's arm. Together they laugh at Dee.

"And I left my wife in England for this?"

"Yes, strange choice, Doctor Dee," replies Samuel.

Suddenly there is a knock on the front door. Martha opens the door. Outside stand a peasant and his wife.

Samuel walks to the door.

"Please, sir, help us," says the peasant.

"How can I help you?" asks Samuel.

"My wife is barren, and we want a child."

"Have you no children?"

"None," replies the peasant. "We've tried for years. You're our last hope."

"I'm your last 'hope'?" Samuel says as he shakes his head in disapproval. "Then, no, there's nothing I can do for you."

Samuel turns and walks away. Dee walks up to him.

"But surely, Samuel, there must be..."

Samuel glares at him, which causes Dee to cut his sentence short. The peasant becomes more desperate and walks up to them.

"But it's said that you have the Elixir." The peasant holds out some gold coins to Samuel. "We are poor, but will give you all we've saved. Please, sir, just a little to make her fertile."

"No, you don't understand. It's not a question of money." Samuel turns towards the peasant's wife. "Woman, your husband says that I'm your last hope. Is that true?"

"No," she answers, "if you cannot help us, then we

will try again. Somehow, some way, we will try again."
Samuel nods his head in agreement as he softly strokes
his beard with his hand.

"Yes. But you must understand. This is very danger-
ous. It might cost you your life. Only the purest souls
may drink without fear. Are you willing to take such a
risk?"

"Yes," says the peasant's wife.

"Then wait here."

Samuel goes into a side room. After a few moments
he returns, carrying a glass vial. The vial contains a
clear crystalline liquid that sparkles when held up to
the light. Samuel carries it to a table in the center of
the room. On the table lies a lead spoon and a bouquet of flowers. Samuel removes the glass stopper
from the vial. As he does this a bit of the Elixir drops
from the stopper onto the flowers. Immediately they
blossom and grow to full bloom before the eyes of the
amazed viewers. Dee picks one of the flowers from
the bouquet and admires it.

Samuel pours a very small portion from the vial onto
the lead spoon. He approaches the peasant's wife.

"Drink this."

He places the Elixir to her lips. She takes it into her
mouth and swallows it. After a few moments her body
begins to emit a soft, golden glow. Samuel places the
spoon back on the table next to the vial. Dee stares at

it with amazement as the lead spoon turns into gold. Dee touches Samuel's arm and turns to the gold spoon. Samuel looks at the spoon but ignores it and Dee as he watches the peasant's wife. Dee picks up the spoon.

"How do you feel?"

"Full with life," replies the peasant's wife.

Samuel turns to the peasant. "Now go home and love your wife." The peasant is overjoyed.

"Thank you, sir, thank you!" he says as they exit.

Dee approaches Samuel with both the flower and gold spoon in his hand.

"Samuel, this Elixir. What is this potion? How does it work?"

"Once you take of the Elixir," replies Samuel, "you become whatever you desire to be. Be it for good...or evil."

It is twilight. As the sun sets the moon begins to rise. Wolves bay to the silvery sphere in the evening sky. Battle horns lift up against the night as bassoon-like sounds fill the air. Thundering hoofbeats of horses are heard as they gallop through the forest. A band of soldiers rides through the night. They are lead by a huge man dressed in blood-red armor. Behind him rides Fontune the magician. He's dressed in a black cape that flows behind him in the wind. They are followed by pagan soldiers, whose armor and head-gear are decorated with animalistic and bestial images.

Samuel and Martha sit in front of the fire, with Dee at their side. Suddenly Samuel hears the baying of the wolves. He quickly stands up and intently listens.

"No, he wouldn't dare," says Samuel.

"Who? What?" asks Dee.

Samuel becomes very disturbed as he continues to listen to the night sounds. Then suddenly he becomes very sad.

"The fool."

Martha takes his arm. "What is it, Samuel?"

"Monde...and Fontune."

"Monde?" asks Dee.

"Yes, Monde. A demon who hates peace and loves strife. Quickly, the two of you must leave." Martha protests. "No, Samuel, I won't leave you."

"You must," he says placing his hand on her pregnant belly. "For our child's sake."

He then turns to Dee. "There's not much time. You came for knowledge and that you shall have. But first, if anything happens to me, you must care for my wife and soon to be born son. Within six months after his twenty-first birthday he'll return for the Elixir, and then you'll receive all the answers you need. But go now." He opens the front door and points to the mountains. "There, up through that pass."

Martha embraces Samuel. They kiss. Samuel then reaches inside his shirt and takes off an amulet. It's made of gold and has an opening in its center. He hands the amulet to Dee.

"When the child is born, place this around his neck. It will bring him the love and protection he'll need."

Samuel embraces Martha once more, then watches as she and Dee quickly start towards the mountains. After a few moments he closes the door, then quickly goes into the side room.

Samuel walks to a dresser, on which stands a box. He opens the box and takes out the glass vial containing the Elixir. Samuel then utters some incantations. The Elixir then slowly levitates off the table and floats in the air towards him, as it begins to sparkle and glow. Samuel walks in a circle around it.

"Stay hidden until called for by my worthy son."

Suddenly the air around the vial begins to swirl and break apart into a stream of brilliant colors. The vial starts to turn within this vortex of pastels, then spins faster and faster until, like a magnet, it draws all the colors of the rainbow onto its surface. It then suddenly disappears into another dimension, as Samuel stands alone in the room. The loud sounds of hoofbeats are heard outside the hut. Suddenly the door is pushed open as two soldiers enter the room. They seize Samuel and drag him out of the hut.

The sun is quickly setting on the horizon as Dee and Martha climb up the slopes. Martha suddenly cries out in pain as she falls to the ground. Dee rushes to help her as she starts to give birth to her child. Dee looks down into the valley below. In the distance he can see smoke rising from Samuel's hut.

Samuel stands in front of the burning hut. His arms are tied behind his back. His furniture and possessions from the hut are strewn on the ground around him. The sky is filled with red flames as black smoke covers the last golden rays of the setting sun. The warrior in red armor rides up to Samuel.

"The Elixir, old man. Your life for the Elixir."

Samuel turns his face away and ignores him. This angers the red knight, who then draws his sword and points it at Samuel's chest. Fontune rides up to them.

"Wait," yells Fontune, "he wears the amulet around his neck. Get the amulet."

"You betrayed me, boy. I, who taught you everything," says Samuel.

"Yet denied me that which was rightfully mine," shouts Fontune with hatred glaring in his eyes.

"You wouldn't have been able to use it, Fontune," replies Samuel, "because you never learned how to share or trust. In your selfishness you would have destroyed the power; and yourself along with it."

Two warriors approach Samuel. They tear off his shirt and expose his bare chest.

"The amulet," screams Fontune. "Where is it?"

Samuel turns away with contempt. "Enough. Do your worst."

"So be it," snarls the red knight.

Losing his patience, the red knight lifts his sword up in the air. This movement causes Fontune's horse to rear up and turn Fontune away from the knight and Samuel.

"No, wait!" cries out Fontune. But it is too late. The red knight drives his sword into Samuel's chest. Samuel cries out in pain.

The death cries of the dying wizard blend into the birth cries of his newborn son. Dee holds the child in his arms. He takes the amulet from his pocket and places it around the child's neck. Dee then lifts the child up to the sky, betwixt the sun and the moon, while it's still covered with it's mother's birth blood. In the distance, smoke rises from the burning hut of the dead wizard.

The body of Samuel lies on the ground. His blood flows out of him onto the grass. The warriors mockingly laugh at the dead wizard. Fontune stares at the body with fear and regret. He angrily yells at the red knight.

"You've gone too far. There's nothing to be gained in this," says Fontune. The red knight snarls at him as he turns his horse and starts to ride away. The other warriors also walk away from the body and begin to mount their horses.

Suddenly a gale wind starts to blow across the sky. A flock of birds fly up into the air. Clouds speed forth as lightning flashes across the blackened heavens. A storm rises up on the horizon. The earth quakes and begins to rumble. The ground around the dead wizard magically opens up and sucks in his body.

The warriors grumble in amazement and fear as they back away from the spot. The red knight unsheathes his sword as he glares about, ready for any possible attack. Fontune covers his face with his black cloak. Suddenly, the earth again rumbles and opens up on the spot where Samuel died. Here, before the eyes of the frightened soldiers, a small oak tree sprouts up. With full green foliage it grows up to a height of six feet. The red knight rears his horse up as Fontune sweeps his cape across his body in an attempt to hide.

"Cut it down and throw it into the flames," orders the red knight.

Two soldiers attack the tree with their swords. As they strike it the tree screams out in pain. From its cuts flows a blue sap; a blue blood which flows back into the ground around its roots. The warriors fearfully back away. The roots suck in this blue sap, and the tree immediately grows to twice its original size in height, strength and fullness. The warriors mumble in terror as they back farther away from the tree.

"Destroy it," orders the red knight. "Attack the tree. Attack it!"

One warrior refuses and starts to run away. The red knight rides after him and cuts him down with his sword. Four of the warriors then attack the tree and hack it with sword and axe. Again the tree howls in pain and anger, and again the blue sap flows out of its trunk and into the ground. Once more the tree grows double in size and strength, now to a height of twenty-four feet.

Suddenly, from the distance, an eagle flies through the sky and settles on top of the tree. One of the warriors shoots an arrow at the eagle. It flutters its wings, lifts itself off the branch, and catches the arrow in its beak. The eagle then swoops down towards the warriors. It circles over the head of Fontune, then snaps the arrow in two with its beak and lets it fall to the ground in front of him. The eagle then flies back to the top of the tree where it perches.

Lightning flashes against the black sky as the gale winds blow and hurl their fury against the band of soldiers. The warriors huddle together on their horses as they retreat from nature's onslaught.

One of the soldiers raises his sword up to the sky, screams out a battle cry, then charges towards the tree. A bolt of lightning strikes out from the sky and hits the sword. Blue-white energy flows down through the man's armor, electrocuting both him and the horse. Together they light up against the black sky. The earth trembles and rumbles about the soldiers as it swallows them up into a six-foot deep pit. They become entrapped and cannot escape. Lightning bolts strike down into their midst. One armored warrior who is hit by lightning falls onto another warrior and thereby electrocutes them both. Smoke from burning flesh pours out of the pit. The red knight races his horse away from the tree and towards the forest. Fontune follows.

Lightning continues to strike into the pit until the screams of the dying men stop and all their movements cease. The earth then rumbles once more as it swallows them all up. The red knight and Fontune escape. They ride across a ravine; silhouettes against the night sky.

On the mountaintop, Dee holds the child in his arms as he watches the destruction in the valley below. As the clouds disperse, the storm begins to subside and the air calms. Dee then looks to the ground at Martha, who is dying from childbirth. He places the child in her arms. She smiles faintly as she holds onto it.

"A name. The child will need a name," says Dee.

Martha turns her head and looks down into the valley at her burning home. She then turns back to Dee. "Michael. He will be called Michael."

Martha then dies. Dee closes her eyes with his fingertips and takes the child from her arms. He holds him up at arm's length, then sadly speaks to him. "Michael, may your life be more joyous than your birth."

82

Elixir

Dee leans back in his chair upon finishing the story. Michael is amazed by what he has just heard, as are Kelly and Jane.

"Yesterday was your twenty-first birthday. Samuel had told me that within six months of that date you'll return to your homeland, take possession of the Elixir, and then all my questions would be answered." Michael laughs to himself.

"What's so funny?" asks Dee.

"I just realized that Suzanne has run away in order to find me." He then becomes depressed and slouches down in his chair. "Now why are you sad?" asks Jane.

"Because even if find her, she won't recognize me. I have no special powers." He turns back to Dee. "What should I do?"

"My time as teacher is over," responds Dee, but then he remembers the crystal. "The crystal. Your father's spirit said it should be used to answer our questions."

They all look at the crystal with solemn expectation. After a few moments they look back at Dee, who scratches his head in confusion.

"Well, what's wrong?" asks Michael.

"I don't know how to activate it," responds Dee.

"Didn't the spirit give you instructions?" says Kelly.

"He vanished before I could ask," answers Dee.

"Well try something, anything!" says Michael with frustration in his voice.

Dee solemnly approaches the ball, waves his hands over it, then utters an incantation. A long, intense moment passes as everyone waits with anticipation. Nothing happens. A nervous restlessness spreads through the group. Poohfer, who had returned to the lab while Dee was telling the story of Michael's birth, steps forward.

"Perhaps we should place it in water. . ."

Contempt glares in Dee's eyes as he stares at Poohfer, who meekly shuts up and backs away.

"We can't give up hope," says Michael. "Try again."

"I really don't know what to do," says Dee.

Kelly steps forward. "Oh, let me try. I've always had luck with advanced technology."

Kelly picks up the ball and rubs it against his chest as he intensely peers deeply into the crystal. "Come out, come out, whatever you are."

Suddenly, there is a loud thunderclap and a puff of smoke appears in the center of the room. When
84

the smoke clears, Madimi, a six-year old female
cherub, sits sprawled out in the center of the room.
She is naked except for a white linen cloth tied
around her waist. She sits with her legs spread apart
as she picks the lint from her belly-button. She is
completely unaware of the people watching her.
She hums to herself and is very content as she
continues to pick the fluff from her belly.

Dee covers his mouth and loudly coughs. Madimi
hears the sound, looks up and notices the people.
At first she's baffled as she looks around the room.
Then she becomes aware of her nakedness. She
smiles with amusement at the situation, laughs
aloud, then disappears in another puff of smoke.
They all look at each other with expressions of
shock, fear and amazement. There's another puff of
smoke and Madimi reappears sitting on top of Dee's
bookcase. She's now dressed in a pretty pink dress
with lots of white frills. In her blond hair is a pink
bow, which she proudly fiddles. She also holds a
small wand that produces sparkles whenever she
waves it through the air. She continues to hum.
Michael walks towards the cherub and bows to her.

"Spirit, please help me," says Michael.

Madimi is overjoyed at the attention she's getting.
"And what can I do for you?" she replies.

"I want the love of a young woman."

"Oh," she says with disappointment, "and this time

I thought that it might be something interesting. You look handsome enough to win her on your own."

"I had her, but now she's gone."

"Did you beat her?"

"Why, of course not."

"Well, my specialty lies in joy and pleasure. Young women can be difficult. How about a puppy? Their faithfulness will last a lifetime. "

Michael shakes his head no. Jane steps forward. "What he really needs is proof that he's a wizard's son," says Jane.

Madimi is impressed. "Oh, really."

Dee approaches Madimi. "Madame, how should I address you?" he asks.

"My name is Madimi."

"Madimi, it was prophesied that one day Michael would possess the Elixir," says Dee.

"Oh, then you must have the amulet," replies Madimi.

"Yes. Yes, he does," says Dee. "Show it to her, Michael."

Elixir

"I did have it, but I gave it to Suzanne."

"Well, it's simple, then," responds Madimi. "She has the amulet. Then all you need is the emerald. Together they'll lead you to the Elixir."

"But where is the emerald?" asks Dee.

"In the ruins of a castle that's a few days journey to the east. Finding the castle should be no problem. Getting the emerald is another matter."

"This is all well and good for the Elixir," responds Michael. "But what of Suzanne's love?"

"Well, as I said, my specialty is merriment. To capture a woman's heart you must appeal to the god of love."

"And how do I contact him?" asks Michael.

"He comes not at the call of a name, but only after the solution of a riddle."

With the wave of her wand, Madimi produces the image of a circle in the air. Next to that she produces the image of a straight line. Both the circle and the line float in the air in front of Michael. "Solve the riddle of the circle and the line, and then you'll be able to look upon the face of love." With this Madimi vanishes, leaving the circle and the line, like a trail of smoke, to slowly dissipate in the air.

Michael turns to the others. "Do any of you know the answer to this riddle?" They all shrug.

"Then I must find Suzanne," says Michael.

"The emerald first," says Dee.

"No," replies Michael. "Suzanne first. Then we'll see what happens next. I'll leave now."

"Then go, to Bohemia, and we'll follow in the morning," responds Dee.

Michael quickly leaves the room. Dee sits back down in his chair and gazes at the crystal. "Finally, after all these long years, the things that have been foretold are about to be realized."

The others gather around the table and look at the crystal. Behind it flicker the flames of the furnace.

"To the future," says Dee. "May it lead us all to knowledge."

"And wealth," says Kelly as he fingers the sack of red powder in his hands.

"And happiness," adds Jane, as she puts her hands on Dee's shoulders.

To the side stands Poohfer, who feels separated from the others, and opposite him, on the work-bench, sits the cat.

88

17

The morning light breaks through the windows of Dee's laboratory as he and Poohfer pack boxes and prepare for their journey. Dee is tying string around bundles of books that he intends to take with him. Kelly sits at the table by the crystal ball. Jane has some bags in her hands. She is about to leave the lab.

"I'll take these up to the house for storage," says Jane.

"Fine, fine," answers Dee.

Kelly admiringly winks at Jane as she passes by. She is embarrassed by his actions and hurries out the door. Kelly laughs to himself.

"Finish this last experiment," Dee says to Poohfer, "then pack the rest of the chemicals into the wagon."

Poohfer grumbles to himself as he goes to the furnace.

"And Poohfer, please take care," says Dee.

"Poohfer take care, Poohfer take care," he says to himself in a mocking tone. As he opens the furnace door the cat hisses at him. "Now, don't you start," he says to the cat, "for I know of some dogs who'd like an extra bit of fur for winter." The cat again hisses at him, then slowly backs into a corner without taking his eyes off Poohfer. Poohfer makes believe that he's ignoring the cat as he slowly moves towards it. Then, when he is within close range, he quickly throws a ladle at the cat. It hits him in the rear. The cat shrieks when it's hit. Poohfer lifts his head high with a sense of accomplishment and superiority. He smiles to himself with satisfaction as he sloppily starts mixing some chemicals together.

"Mercury, sulfur and salt," he repeats as he prepares the mixture. He reaches for a canister of salt but instead grabs one labeled, "SALTPETER."

Dee finishes with his books and turns to Kelly.

"Are you sure you won't come along? You seem to be handy with that crystal."

Kelly lifts up his sack of powder. "No, I have all the treasure I need. Just came by to wish you well, and now I'll take my leave."

Kelly then waves goodbye to Dee and starts out the door. But halfway through the door he freezes, for there, coming down the street is Ann, the constable, and the two priests, one without a cap, walking towards the laboratory. Kelly gulps, then quickly ducks back into the room. He slams the door shut behind him and quickly surveys the room. His eyes lock onto a large wicker basket.

"Back so soon?" asks Dee.

Kelly runs to the wicker basket, lifts the cover, then hops in. "Remember thy virtues, Dee. Loyalty to thy friends is foremost. Loyalty!"

Kelly then sinks into the basket and puts the cover back on top.

In the street outside, Ann and the constable are having an argument.

"Don't you worry, daughter. I'll find him," says the constable.

"Well, make sure you do!" she answers.

Ann reveals a streak of meanness by pulling on her father's hair and bending back two of his fingers. The constable cries out in pain and raises his arm up to strike her. But his arm freezes in midair as Ann glares at him with a defiant look signaling all hell would break loose if he dared hit her. She pulls back her fist as she readies to strike him back.

"What, strike a woman?" asks one of the priests.

The two priests are aghast and cast reprimanding stares at the constable. This causes him to lower his arm. He grumbles and turns away as the priests nod approvingly. The constable then kicks in the door to Dee's lab. It slams against the wall as it barely stays on its hinges. He then enters the room, followed by Ann and the two priests.

"Yes, can I help you?" asks Dee.

"We're looking for a man named Kelly," answers the constable.

"Reverend Kelly," adds Ann.

The constable begins to survey the lab in his search for Kelly. "There is reason to believe that Kelly is pretending to be a man of the cloth."

"An imposter, and a thief, too," says one of the priests.

"Of a young woman's virtue," adds Ann.

"And high level...material things," says the priest without the cap.

"And thereby defaming the good image of the church," adds the other priest.

In his tour of the lab the constable has arrived at the wicker basket in which Kelly is hiding. He sits down on top of the basket.

"Do you know the whereabouts of this man?" asks the constable.

"Not if he's right beneath you," answers Dee.

The constable looks down to the floor by his feet, sees nothing, then begins to laugh. His great bulk shakes with laughter. This causes him to inadvertently "pass wind" into the wicker basket. He becomes embarrassed.

"Excuse me," he says, "it's a bad lower tract."

He then stands up, coughs, and begins to wave the air with his hat. The odor is so bad that the constable himself has to walk away from the wicker basket.

"Gentlemen and lady," says Dee, "as you can see, I'm about to leave on journey."

"Yes," responds the constable," but you must understand our situation. I have a daughter here that must be done right by. If you see him, tell him of our concerns."

"That I promise," answers Dee.

"Then good day to you, sir," say the priests.

"And to you all," answers Dee. The constable, Ann and the priests leave the lab. Dee tries to close the door behind them, but because of the recent damage when the constable kicked it in, the bottom of the door drags across the floor. Finally he gets it closed, but now it's stuck in the jam. He bolts it.

"Damn, I'll fix it when we get back." Dee looks towards the wicker basket and calls out to Kelly. "You can come out now, they're all gone."

But there is no movement from the basket. Dee starts towards the basket but becomes revolted by the odor and backs away. "Poohfer!" he calls out.

Poohfer, who has watched the whole episode, stares at Dee with disbelief. He then shakes his head in rejection and starts to walk out of the room in the opposite direction.

"Come here, man! Thy livelihood's at stake!!" yells Dee.

Poohfer angrily walks to the furnace, opens its door, throws in the pot containing the sulfur-saltpeter mixture, then slams the furnace door shut. The furnace has not yet been relit. Poohfer then walks to the basket. He gags from the odor, but succeeds in removing the top as he topples over the basket. Kelly rolls out. He is gassed, but semi-conscious. Poohfer returns to the furnace. He is disgruntled.

"You tell me to do one thing, then another. Mix mercury, sulfur, and salt..."

Dee is trying to revive Kelly. "Well, forget it now, I've already packed the salt."

Poohfer becomes self-righteous. "No, you haven't already packed the salt." Then under his breath he mumbles, "Dumb old goat." Poohfer then walks back to the counter and retrieves the canister. The cat sees him coming and jumps into a pail for protection. He then looks out from under the pail as Poohfer prances about.

"Moron," screams Dee. "I know what I do!"

Kelly finally becomes revived. Dee helps him stand up.

"You heard it all?" asks Dee.

"Methinks the fresh air of Bohemia would do me well."

Poohfer walks up to Dee and hands him the canister. He then speaks to Dee in a mocking tone of voice.

"Well, forget it then, I've already packed the salt." He then returns to the furnace and takes some matches from his pocket.

"It's not bad enough that I have to prepare these stupid experiments, but now he wants me to waste my efforts," mumbles Poohfer as he opens the furnace door.

Dee stares at the label, then reacts with horror. Kelly sees his expression, then quickly reads the label.

"Saltpeter," says Kelly.

"And sulphur," adds Dee.

Kelly shrugs his shoulders. "Makes gunpowder. Elementary chemistry."

"Cooking in the furnace," babbles Dee, as his eyes bulge in terror.

Poohfer has just finished lighting the furnace. He closes its door, blows out the match, then places the smoking match into a glass of water. "Safety first," he says to himself as he crosses his arms on his chest with self-satisfaction.

Dee quickly runs to the door. He struggles with it but can't open the door because it's stuck. Kelly, who has suddenly realized the gravity of the situation, screams out in terror as he runs towards the window. The cat jumps out from under the pail and scurries around the room. Poohfer stares at them with puzzlement.

"Hey, what's the matter?"

Kelly dives through the window just as the gunpowder explodes, with the cat jumping out right behind him. The force of the explosion blows the door off the hinges with Dee still holding onto it. A big billow of black smoke flows out of the doorway into the street. Poohfer then walks out of the lab with black soot all over his face and body, with his clothes in complete shreds.

18

Michael is walking down the street of a European village when he notices an old woman being tormented by some small children. They are throwing pebbles at her as she carries a load of supplies in a sack on her back. Michael chases the children away.

"Here now, you stop that!" he yells at them.

The children run away. The old woman smiles at Michael in appreciation. "No respect for the old nowadays. They make me the target for their jests."

"You'll be safe now," Michael replies as he turns to leave.

"Where are you going?"

"I'm searching for a young woman."

"Ah, then no time for an old lass like me. But maybe I could be of help."

"I think not...but then? Do you know the meaning of the circle and the line?"

"What's that?"

"A riddle."

"I'm no good at riddles, but I know those who are."

"Who?"

"In yonder forest...there." She points towards a dark forest in the distance. "A band of elves and fairies make it their home."

"Do you think they'd help me?"

The old woman lays down her load and takes two cakes from her sack. "Offer them some of these, and take a bite yourself, for them the better to see." She laughs, picks up her sack, and leaves.

19

Suzanne is walking through a village market as she surveys the merchandise in the various booths. She walks by three gypsies. They admire her and watch to see if she's alone. Satisfied that she is, one of them continues to follow her as the other two run up ahead. The gypsy goes up to Suzanne.

"Would you like to see some beautiful pearls?"

"Pearls? I love pearls. Where?" answers Suzanne.

"In the tent, there." He points to a tent that is just a few feet in front of them.

"Sure, why not?"

"But perhaps we should wait for your friends?"

"Oh no, I'm traveling alone."

The gypsy smiles at her. "Then come." He leads her forward. As he enters the tent, he indicates to the other two gypsies that she is alone.

Inside the tent there is no display of pearls, just a pile of rugs on the floor. Suzanne turns to the gypsy.

"Where are the pearls?"

He takes her hand. "Within the depths of your eyes."

Suzanne suddenly realizes what is going on. She tries to pull back her hand, but the gypsy holds it tighter as he laughs. The other two men take a step towards her. Suzanne puts her hand to her mouth and giggles. She smiles at the three gypsies and then giggles some more. They all smile back at her. Then quickly she punches the first gypsy in the mouth and knocks him across the tent. She then opens her mouth up wide as she readies to let out an enormous scream. One of the other gypsies quickly puts his hand into her mouth. Her jaws snap down on the hand. This forces the man down to his knees as he attempts to muffle his groans of pain. The other two gypsies join the scuffle as they quickly jump on her. They gag her, then tie her up. They lay her down on the floor and quickly roll her up in one of the rugs. Two of them then pick up the rug and carry it to the tent's entrance.

A lone gypsy exits the tent and looks about the marketplace. Satisfied that they are not being watched, he motions for the other two gypsies to come out. They exit, carrying the rug that contains Suzanne on their shoulders. The three of them meander through the crowd away from the marketplace.

20

Dee, Jane, Kelly and Poohfer ride in a wagon through the countryside. Dee sits in the front seat and reads a book as he drives. To the right of him sits Jane. Kelly is in the back of the wagon behind Jane. He's whittling a piece of wood. At the far end of the wagon sits Poohfer, and across from him the cat. They stare at each other in mutual animosity. The wagon rocks back and forth as it travels over the old country road. Kelly whittles away at the stick as he continuously tries to catch Jane's eye. Finally, she turns and looks down at him. He smiles, holds the stick erect, then takes it to his lips and slightly blows on it.

"A flute," he says.

"Aye, I can see that," replies Jane.

Kelly then lays the stick down in his lap. Suddenly the wagon hits a bump that knocks Jane out of her seat and into Kelly's lap. Kelly wraps his arms around Jane and takes every advantage possible in the situation. Dee looks back and sees Jane sitting in Kelly's lap.

"Are you all right, Jane?" asks Dee. He holds out his hand. Jane takes it, then Dee pulls her back up to her seat. He then looks down at the wooden wheels.

"The ride can get rough on these wooden spokes," says Dee.

"It can make a man stiff," says Kelly as he stretches his back.

"And cause a woman to remember more pleasurable drives," adds Jane as she smiles at Kelly.

21

Michael munches on one of the cakes given to him by the old woman as he enters the forest. The foliage is larger than the normal size. As Michael walks past a large leaf, he awakens an elf sleeping under it. The elf follows Michael.

As Michael continues to walk, the foliage becomes denser and larger. Rainbow-colored birds squawk and sing loudly as they swoop by him. The elf behind Michael is now joined by a fairy who flies lightly in the air. Finally Michael reaches a babbling brook in the middle of a forest. He sits down and drinks from the stream. When he finishes, he looks up and sees that he's surrounded by fairies. He falls back to the ground in amazement.

"What are you doing here?" asks the elf.

"I have a riddle," declares Michael.

The fairies all giggle and flutter about. "And so do we, so do we!" they all exclaim.

"Do you know the answer to the riddle?" asks the elf.

"No, but I was told that you might help me."

"For what in return?"

Michael holds up the cakes. The fairies again giggle, then swoop down and quickly gobble up all of them.

"What's the riddle, what's the riddle?" they all ask.

"What is the meaning of the circle and the line?"

"Ah, a question of love," answers the elf.

"I was told by a spirit that I should seek out the god of love."

"But only after you've solved the riddle will he come," replies the elf. "And pray tell, sir, can you stare into the sun?"

The elf points up the bright sun above them. Michael tries to look into it but the pain forces him to cover his eyes. The elf laughs.

"If you're not pure enough to look at this sphere above, then how could you ever hope to gaze on love?"

The fairies flutter around and nod their heads in agreement. The elf continues to laugh.

"So what makes you think you'd have that might?" asks the elf.

"I've been told the Elixir's my birthright," answers Michael.

The elf jumps back and the fairies ecstatically flutter about Michael.

"Then he should be able to regain the emerald," says

104

one of the fairies. "Yes, yes, the emerald!" cry out the other fairies.

"It once belonged to our realm," says the elf, "but was stolen by a wizard's son. Return it to us and we'll lead you to the Solwoes. They are the guardians of the god of love."

"And where am I to find this emerald?" asks Michael.

"In the castle ruins, far beyond those hills," respond the fairies, as they point at a distant mountain range to the east.

22

The three gypsies, still carrying the rug on their shoulders, enter the gypsy campsite. They place the rug on the ground as the other gypsies gather about. They then quickly roll it open. Suzanne tumbles out and rolls across the ground in the dirt. Everyone laughs at her. Then two of the men pick her up and tie her to a post. Suddenly the crowd becomes quiet as the gypsy king comes out of his wagon. He is a fat, brutal-looking man. He walks up to Suzanne, takes her chin in his hand, and smiles at her. He's missing two front teeth, which gives him a repulsive grin. Suzanne turns away with revulsion. The king laughs loudly, shouts something in an unintelligible language, then walks away. The crowd roars with laughter and approval.

A young gypsy girl comes up to Suzanne with a canteen of water. She removes the gag from Suzanne's mouth and pours her a drink.

"Here, have some water," says the girl.

As Suzanne takes a sip from the canteen, a vicious fight breaks out among two of the gypsies who had kidnapped her.

"Why are they fighting?" asks Suzanne.

"To decide who'll have you first tonight," answers the girl. Suzanne chokes on the water and spits it out.

106

"That is," continues the gypsy girl, "after our king." She points to the toothless king, who in turn smiles at them.

23

Dee's wagon is parked under a tree, as Dee and Kelly sit near the campfire. It's twilight. Dee has the crystal ball in his lap and is trying to activate it, but to no avail.

"It's no good, says Dee. "I rub it like you do, hold it close to my body, yet still there is no effect."

"Perhaps it has something to do with our natures," responds Kelly. Kelly then takes the ball and places it in his lap. He tenderly rubs his hands around it. Jane walks up to the two men and gives them both something to drink.

"Thank you," says Kelly.

Jane smiles softly and lingers a moment too long before she moves on. Kelly softly smiles to himself as he drinks from the cup.

"Let's try to contact Madimi again," says Dee.

"All right," answers Kelly.

Kelly begins to concentrate as he rubs on the ball. Once again Madimi appears in a puff of white smoke. Dee approaches her as he speaks in a formal tone of voice.

"Madame, I wish to address a question to you."

Madimi is put off by his formality and glares at him with contempt. She sees Jane standing alone by the tent, as Poohfer busies himself by the wagon. Madimi then briskly walks over to Kelly and bends down to whisper something in his ear.

Dee becomes indignant. "Madame, it is my ball!"

Madimi lifts up the flap on Kelly's cap and notices that he is missing an ear.

"How did that happen?"

Kelly lowers his head to the ground and mumbles.

"Well, never mind," says Madimi. "I can fix it, if you do me a favor."

Kelly perks up. "Anything, anything."

With a wave of her wand Madimi brings back Kelly's ear. He tears off the priest's cap and becomes over-whelmed with happiness. She then whispers into his ear. A look of surprise comes across Kelly's face, then a smile of immense pleasure, which is followed by an expression of guilt. Madimi steps back and together she and Kelly look at Jane. Madimi nods her head in reaffirmation. Kelly then looks over at Dee and gulps, as Madimi disappears in a puff of smoke. Dee approaches him.

"What did she say?"

Kelly hesitates. "Um..."

"Well, come on, out with it."

"Madimi refuses to answer any more of your questions unless..."

"Unless what?" asks Dee.

Kelly gulps. "Unless you consent to share...Jane with me."

"What!!! Preposterous!!!" says Dee. He stomps around in confusion and disbelief. Jane has not heard a word of what's been said. She continues to work with Poohfer by the wagon. Dee scratches his head as he sits down next to Kelly. He's uncertain as what to believe.

"Did she really say that?" he whispers to Kelly.

Kelly nods his head yes. There is a long pause as both men ponder their situations.

"You know what I think?" says Kelly.

"What?"

"It's a test of your faith."

"No," responds Dee, but then after a pause, "you really think so?"

"Think about it," says Kelly, "and the knowledge you hope to gain. This was a heavenly spirit that brought the crystal to you."

Dee nods his head in agreement. "And it's not like you're making this up. I saw her here myself, just now, and she did heal your ear."

110

"And would I be one to betray a friend?"

Dee ponders this, then warily stares at Kelly, who in turn gulps and quickly starts to speak.

"Well, think of it this way. Compared to the trials of Job, and the tests put to Abraham...how difficult could this be?" Dee ponders the comparison.

24

As Michael reaches the top of a mountain peak, the sun sets on the horizon. In the distance he sees the ruins of a castle and begins to walk in that direction.

Michael stands among the castle ruins, looking for an entrance. Suddenly a flock of bats fly out of an opening and attack him. He covers his head, picks up a stick, and beats away the bats. After they have all dispersed, he cautiously enters the opening. Inside the ruins it is very dark. Michael sees a torch hanging on the side of the wall. He pulls it off and lights it. He then continues down the passageway. As he turns the corner, he becomes entangled within a massive spider web. Large black spiders begin to descend along the web towards him. Michael struggles to release himself as the spiders come closer and closer. Beads of sweat pour from his forehead. He defends himself as the spiders come closer and closer. Beads of sweat pour from his forehead. He defends himself by attacking the spiders with his torch. They back away from the flames, but then the web catches on fire. Michael fights to free himself, and finally falls away to the floor as the flames lick up the web along the walls and ceiling of the cavern. Burning spiders fall to the ground, bats screech and swoop through the hallway, and large rats scurry across the floor in order to escape the flames. Michael keeps the creatures away from him by striking at them with his lighted torch.

Finally the blaze subsides. Michael then continues down the hallway until he reaches a large open room. He turns around and walks backwards as he tries to view the room in its entirety. He bumps into something, then turns around to see a decayed skull with empty eye sockets staring at him. The skeleton lies on its back and has a long sword driven into its chest. A small snake twists around the sword and the skeleton's ribs, as two small rats scurry out of the chest cavity. Michael quickly backs away with horror. After a pause to catch his breath, he sees another opening in the wall and starts towards it. Michael walks into the room. On the remains of a table he sees the emerald, a beautiful large green gem glowing in the dark. Unbeknownst to Michael, on the wall behind him, stands the petrified form of Fontune the magician, who had been frozen into the rock wall. As Michael slowly approaches the emerald, the form of Fontune slowly transforms from its solid state and becomes human once again. When Michael touches the emerald, Fontune opens his eyes. Michael cautiously puts his hands around the emerald and lifts it up from the table. By this time Fontune is completely transformed back into a human. As Michael admires the beauty of the emerald, Fontune moves away from the wall. Michael hears a sound behind him, turns, and is startled to see Fontune. Michael jumps back with fright as he drops the emerald from his hands. With a wave of his hand Fontune stops the emerald's fall before it hits the floor. It hovers in the air. Then with a slow movement of his right hand he moves the emerald in the air towards him. Michael dives for it but with the flick of his wrist the emerald pops into Fontune's hands. Michael misses and crashes to the floor. Michael gets up and angrily charges towards Fontune, but with a mere wave of his hand Fontune sends the boy flying across the room, and slams Michael up against the other wall. An energy force flows from Fontune's hand. It hits Michael in the chest and pins him against the wall.

"And who are you?" bellows Fontune.

Michael doesn't respond. Fontune tears off Michael's shirt and exposes his bare chest.

"Nothing! Just a poor peasant who has wandered beyond his realm. Then to your fate."

Fontune emits a beam of energy from his forehead. When it reaches Michael's wrist the energy transforms into chains which manacle Michael's hands to the wall. Fontune laughs, then transforms himself into a black raven. The raven flies out of the room. Rats scurry across the floor, as spiders and snakes begin to slither along the ground towards Michael.

25

A low campfire burns in the center of the gypsy camp-site. A crowd of gypsies sit around the fire as they drink wine and play musical instruments. At the end of the clearing stands a tent. The light from the fires strikes the tent in such a way that a woman's silhou-ette is projected on the canvas: the figure of a woman inside is having her clothes removed by two other female silhouettes. They bath her body with cloths and dry her off with towels as the men by the camp-fire drink their wine and watch.

Inside the tent, Suzanne stands in the center with her wrists tied to post above her head. The gypsy girl is putting a simple dress on her. The dress falls over Suzanne's shoulders and down along the side of her body until it reaches her ankles.

An old woman enters the tent, the same one who had given Michael the cakes and directed him to the for-est. The gypsy girls respectfully bow down to her. She approaches Suzanne and puts her hand on her face. Suzanne spiritedly turns her head away.

"Good," says the old woman, "the young bucks will enjoy breaking this filly." She then turns to the other girls. "Has she any possessions?"

"Just this," answers the gypsy girl as she holds up the amulet.

The old woman stares at the amulet with shock and fear. She takes it from the girl and holds it in front of Suzanne's face.

"Where did you get this?" she asks Suzanne.

"It was a gift."

The woman becomes very concerned. "Leave us," she orders the girls. They quickly exit the tent. The woman then takes out a knife and approaches Suzanne. She then quickly cuts the ropes that bind her hands. She points to the table.

"Sit down," she orders. Suzanne obeys.

The old woman takes out a deck of Tarot cards and places them in front of Suzanne.

"Handle them! Quickly." Suzanne shuffles the cards. After a few moments the old woman takes them back and begins to lay the cards out on the table.

"What do they say?" asks Suzanne.

"That you are to marry the rightful owner of this amulet, a great and powerful wizard."

"Michael?" Suzanne says with confusion and disbelief.

26

Michael, still chained to the wall, regains consciousness as a large snake slithers across the floor toward his feet. Michael sees the snake, then shouts out.

"Madimi, help me! Madimi!"

The large snake circles around Michael's feet and lifts its head to strike. But suddenly Madimi appears, and with the flick of her wand forces the snake to completely encircle Michael's feet then bite its own tail. Then, with another movement of her wand, she incinerates the snake with flames. Madimi then yawns from boredom.

"Madimi, help me out of these chains."

"How did you get into them?"

"A magician did this. I had the emerald in my hands, but then he stole it from me and locked me in these chains."

"You touched the emerald?"

"Yes."

"Then, Michael, awaken the powers within you, for if shackled by magic, use magic to set yourself free."

As Madimi touches Michael on his forehead with her

wand, a burst of sparkles falls from its tip.

"Now remove the chains that bind thee," she says.

Michael struggles with the chains, but to no avail. Madimi shakes her head in disapproval.

"Not with your body," she says, "but with your mind."

As Michael concentrates, a waveform of electrical energy flows from his forehead towards the chains. Michael intensifies the energy flow until finally the manacles disintegrate.

"Yes," says Madimi, "rather easy once you have the knack. Have you solved the riddle?"

"The fairies said they would help me if I returned the emerald to them."

"And now you failed at that, too."

Michael looks to the floor with dejection. Madimi takes pity on him.

"I'll help by giving you a hint. Are they equal, or unequal?"

"Why unequal, of course," answers Michael.

"Is that so? Think on it some more. But now return above, for the spirit of you father wishes to speak with you."

With that Madimi disappears. Michael looks up and sees a large hole in the ceiling. He then begins to climb up some columns towards the opening.
118

27

The gypsy king struts out of his wagon dressed in his finest clothes. He takes a long swig from a bottle of whisky, then throws the bottle into the campfire. The glass shatters against the stones as flames flare up from the alcohol. A large grin stretches across his face, and he laughs uproariously as he struts towards the tent. A young woman's silhouette is projected against the tent's surface The gypsy king reaches the tent and pulls open the front flaps.

In the center of the tent stands not Suzanne, but the young gypsy girl. The old woman sits at the table with the Tarot cards still spread out in front of her. The king notices that a long hole has been cut into the back wall of the tent. A breeze blows the flaps around the opening. The king angrily glares at the old woman.

"Forget her," shouts the old woman, "lest we be caught up in her fate." The king looks at the Tarot cards on the table. The center card shows a castle tower being struck by lightning.

Outside, in the forest, lightning flashes across the sky as torrents of rain fall from the storm clouds. Suzanne runs through the forest, away from the lights of the campfires in the gypsy camp. She runs through branches and small shrubs that block her path. She trips, falls, and becomes entangled in the underbrush.

After a struggle she breaks free and runs again, until finally the lights can no longer be seen. She falls down in exhaustion as the rains wash over her.

28

Fontune remembers his past as he rides across the plains...Inside the red knight's castle the interior is cave-like and lit by torches which hang upon the walls. Rocks and sharp razor-like edges protrude into the opening. The red knight storms into the room. He angrily throws his shield against the wall. It crashes into the rocks, then clatters when it hits the stone floor. Three sensual women approach him and try to soothe his anger with their caresses, but he just brushes them aside as he furiously paces about. One of the women pours him a cup of wine. He quickly gulps it down, then throws the cup to the floor as Fontune enters the room. "Fool, you've destroyed everything! If my horse hadn't reared and turned me about I could have stopped you," yells Fontune. The red knight reacts with rage. He pulls out his sword. Fontune steps back. The red knight then grips the sword by the handle and throws it at Fontune as if it were a spear. Fontune quickly moves his hands about in a ritualistic manner, which causes the sword to stop in midflight. Fontune moves his hands again. The sword hovers for a moment, then reverses its direction and speeds back towards the red knight. He leans back against the bed as the sword stops an inch from his throat. Fontune continues to hold his arms in their magical position, as the red knight remains frozen with fear. Then, as Fontune slowly lets his arms fall, the sword drops to the floor. They silently stare at each other for a few moments, then Fontune turns and leaves the room.

Fontune enters a side room which is filled with magical apparatus: charts of the heavens, spheres and globes. He raises his arms to the ceiling and utters an incantation. The rock ceiling separates to reveal the star-filled night sky. Fontune walks past a telescope to a desk. He takes the emerald from his pocket and holds it in front of him.

"So close. But when placed within the amulet the Elixir will be mine." Fontune grasps the emerald in his fist. "Then I'll hold the greatest power, and never again will be forced to bow before man or god." He places the emerald down on the table. "But a new way must be found, some new method...a new plan."

He sits down and begins to look through some old charts and books that lie on the desk. He sits with his back to the opening in the ceiling. A blazing comet speeds across the night sky. Its tail becomes longer as it speeds closer to the opening. It then transforms into a ball of fire as it falls through the hole in the ceiling and into the study. Fontune becomes blinded as the room becomes ablaze with light. He leans against the wall and covers his eyes with arms. The whirlwind of fire recedes towards its center as a form begins to materialize in the blackness of the core. This black core grows until finally it takes the shape of Monde. He sneers at Fontune.

"The Elixir?"

"Samuel is dead," replies Fontune.

"Fool, don't talk to me of temporal transformations.

I asked about the Elixir."

"I said the wizard is dead, and the Elixir with him."

"And a tree rose to take his place! What do you think will be the cost of your failure?" asks Monde.

"I didn't kill him!"

The laughter of the red knight is heard from the adjoining room.

"His stupidity will be dealt with shortly," says Monde. "And what of the amulet?"

"Even that was not to be found."

Monde laughs at Fontune with contempt. Fontune becomes angry.

"If your powers are so great what need do you have of me?" asks Fontune.

"Silence. I'll have none of your insolence."

"Then don't mock me, for I've waited long for this prize."

Monde glares at him with contempt. "You've waited long? Your years are but brief moments in the scheme of things. There are rules that cannot be broken, even by me. Because of your failure we must all wait."

"Then wait alone, for I'll not wait with you," replies Fontune.

"Much too late for that. The battle for the Elixir must be fought on the human level. We are partners. Once entered, the contract forever binds. But I've treated you much too kindly. Now that will change!"

The air swirls around Monde as a mist envelops him. As Monde's body transforms, a leering smile remains on his face, until finally this smile changes into the hissing fangs of a snake. The snake spits venom into Fontune's eyes.

Fontune cries out in pain as he falls back against the wall. With a wave of his hand Monde freezes Fontune and makes him part of the rock wall. He then picks up the emerald and rubs his hands over it as he stares at Fontune.

"Sleep, until another comes for this jewel."

He then places the emerald back onto the table. Monde again hears the laughter of the red knight coming form the next room. He slowly dematerializes.

The red knight is drunk as he lies in bed with his three voluptuous women. He rolls onto his back in a drunken stupor, spilling wine on himself and the others as he moves. The women begin to caress him and kiss his body as he throws down his cup and fondles them. A fire burns in the hearth, throwing up a red light that illuminates their lovemaking.

Suddenly the shadow of a tall manlike creature falls across the four people on the bed. They stop all their movements and look towards the source of the shadow, but there is no one to be seen. Yet the shadow remains over them.

The fire in the hearth suddenly goes out. A wind blows through the room and extinguishes most of the torches. In fear, the red knight pushes the women off him as he reaches for his sword. He grabs its handle, then screams out in pain as it becomes seared to his flesh. His hand begins to melt and disintegrate.

The women jump off the bed and scream with horror as the sword begins to move by a force of its own. The sword moves upright. The red knight continues to cry in agony as the flesh melts off his arm. Suddenly the sword reverses its direction and drives itself through the heart of the red knight. The flesh of his chest becomes seared with the heat of the sword, as his torso begins to melt and disintegrate into the bed. The women scream and run in horror as the cavern begins to quake and crumble about them. The floor to the room opens up as the walls of the castle collapse.

Emannon walks along the balcony of the main room of her castle. Watching her from behind a column stands Monde, in his human form. He takes a step forward in order to have a better view. Emannon hears the sound of the footsteps and turns. Because of the darkness she can only see a figure in the shadows. She smiles, believing it to be Fontune.

"Fontune," she says as she starts towards Monde, with her arms opened wide. Monde then steps out from the shadows and smiles at her. Emannon freezes in her tracks as Monde extends his hands towards her.

"Come," says Monde, "I'm sure I'll be able to fill your arms."

"Leave, for I have no desire to be with you."

"No," says Monde with determined resolution.

Emannon turns and quickly runs out of the room as Monde slowly walks after her.

Emannon enters her bedroom and locks the door behind her. She leans against it as she trembles with fear. Suddenly Monde walks through the wall opposite the door. Emannon becomes hysterical as Monde approaches her. She runs from him toward her four-post bed. She falls to her knees and clings to one of the posts in desperation.

"Fontune!" she cries out in desperation.

"He can't hear you," answers Monde.

His shadow creeps over her as Monde reaches out to touch her face.

"So beautiful," he says. "If I were born a woman with your beauty I could rule the world. Men would give everything, just to be near my side, to do my every bidding. For that reason I do hate thee with passion and must possess you." As Monde's fingers touch her face, Emannon becomes cold and disassociates herself from what is about to happen. With a cold, calm indifference she turns her face away from him.

As Monde leans forward his shadow covers Emannon in complete darkness. Only the light of the tall candle on the nightstand remains as it casts flickering shadows against the wall.

The candle has burnt down to but an inch above the table top. Emannon's clothes lay scattered about the floor and the sheets are strewn across the bed. Emannon stand near the window. She is now dressed in a sheer nightgown. Still withdrawn, her mind is no longer concerned with her immediate condition. Monde moves towards her, but she doesn't react. He touches her arm, but she still doesn't acknowledge his presence.

"Much I can teach you. Many powers I can place within your control. Watch."

Some small clay animal figurines, a lion and a bear, stand on a nearby table. Monde picks them up and utters an incantation as he rubs them between his hands. He then places them on the table. The small creatures then become animated and obey Monde's commands.

He puts his hand on her forehead and utters another incantation.

"This power I give you," he says, but there is still no response. "So stonelike. Consent to my desires."

"Why?" she asks. "Earlier you had need for my consent. Your strength sufficed."

"Melt, and I'll give you secrets that will make your beauty eternal."

Emannon turns away from him once again.

"Very well, but think on it, and when you're ready I'll return."

With that Monde disappears. Emannon now relaxes her body, but her soul possesses a hardness that wasn't there before.

"Fontune, I trusted you. You were my protector. But your greed for power led you to abandon me. Now I'm alone and must live without you. Then so be it."

She walks to the dresser on which stands the remains of the once tall candle. On the wall behind the dresser hangs a mirror. Emannon slowly moves her hand over the flame. She holds it there without even flinching as the flames lick at the flesh of her palm. Emannon stares at her face in the mirror. It shows no sign of pain. Slowly she removes her hand from the flame and turns over the palm. The flesh is burnt, yet she still has not shed a tear. Emannon stares at her face in the mirror, then touches a cheek with her fingertips.

"Beauty, tonight a victim you've made me. Henceforth, my weapon you'll be. The Elixir...that which they all seek, I alone shall possess, and with its power all these evils redress."

29

Suzanne walks into an inn that is filled with people eating their dinners. She's hungry, tired, and soaked to the skin from the evening storm. She walks up to the counter. Behind it on the wall is a menu that lists the food selection. Suzanne hungrily stares at the menu. A clerk watches her as she reads through the listing.

"Can I help you?" asks the clerk.

"I'm hungry and I'd like something to eat."

"Fine. What would you like?"

Suzanne hesitates. "There's a problem. I don't have any money. I was robbed by some gypsies."

"You mean you're traveling alone?" asks the clerk with disbelief. "Just a minute. Wait here."

The clerk goes into the kitchen. After a few minutes he returns with the cook, a large mean-looking woman. They both eye Suzanne, then whisper among themselves. Suzanne turns away from them and looks at the crowd in the room. In a far corner she sees two burly ruffians staring at her. They smile at her, but she quickly turns away. The cook comes up to her.

"You can eat if you do some work. Otherwise, go on

your way. You're not family and this isn't a house of charity," says the cook.

"If that's what I have to do to eat, then fine, I'll do it."

"Then into the kitchen with you. First clean the pots, then you'll eat."

Suzanne enters the kitchen after the cook.

30

Flames and shadows flicker against the walls of the dungeon. In the middle of the room is a half-clad alchemist who is tied to a torture rack. The alchemist moans and screams in pain as Grobel, a fat ugly brute, turns the wheel of the rack. Grobel then picks up a stone in one hand and a stick in the other as he approaches the alchemist.

"Speak, Alchemist," says Grobel. "You bragged of your knowledge when you took my coins, so now give up the formula for the Elixir."

"I lied! I have no such knowledge."

Grobel then beats him on the chest with the stone and stick as the alchemist continues to scream out in pain.

"Please stop sir, stop. You're breaking my bones."

Grobel spins around in a fury and in a rage screams at the man. "Well, these are sticks and stones. What did you expect? Weighty arguments? Did you believe I would torture you with...heavy conversation... or...excessive verbiage?" With that, Grobel growls and lashes out at the man by beating him on the chest with the stick and stone. The alchemist again cries out in pain, then loses consciousness. Grobel becomes disgusted with his lack of cooperation, throws down

the stick and stone, picks up a bucket of water, and
dumps the water onto the man's face.

"Come on, up with you!" says Grobel. "I've got work
that's to be done." Grobel shakes the alchemist, but
then realizes that he is dead. He becomes worried.

"Ah...damn it, she's going to be pissed!"

Emannon enters the room. She is still exquisitely beautiful, though hardened by the years. As she walks
towards Grobel, he cowers away from her with fear
and respect. In her hand she carries a short whip and
on her shoulder rides a small monkey. She goes to the
alchemist and then realizes that he is dead. She then
glares at Grobel with contempt.

"Not another one?"

With shame, Grobel lowers his eyes to the floor as his
body droops with dejection.

"I'm sorry," he says, "I just get carried away with my
work."

Emannon quickly lashes out at him with her whip,
as Grobel backs away from her wrath.

"Damn you and your incompetence. Remove him."

Grobel quickly begins to untie the man's legs. The
monkey jumps onto the alchemist's shoulders and
pulls up the dead man's head so as to look into his
face. The monkey then shrieks recriminations of
failure into the dead man's face, then throws the head

back against the rack. It hits with a thud.

Emannon calls out to the monkey. "Come, my pet, he's no longer of any concern to us."

The monkey scurries across the floor and jumps onto Emannon's shoulder. They leave the dungeon.

The monkey watches from a table as Emannon puts the finishing touches on two winged gargoyles that she has constructed out of clay. The gargoyles each stand about five feet tall. They are grotesque creatures that possess wings on their backs, human-like arms and bird-like talons for feet. Each has a sword and shield in its hands.

Emannon puts down her tools and smiles with satisfaction at her work. She doesn't notice a black raven fly into the room and perch upon the top of a column. Emannon raises her arms towards the gargoyles and utters an incantation. She then beams some rays of energy from her forehead onto them. The energy flows into the creatures and gives them life. They snarl and growl as they move about the room. Yet when they approach Emannon they bow and pay homage to her.

"Entertain me! Fight to the death!" she says maliciously.

The gargoyles immediately engage each other in ferocious battle. Sword strikes against sword as each deals the other powerful blows. One cuts off the arm of the other while the second hacks off the leg of the first. They continue to hack each other into mutual annihilation as Emannon and her monkey sit back and laugh.

Finally the gargoyles are nothing but broken pieces of clay on the floor. Emannon then draws the energy that she had given them back into herself. The raven, who had watched the battle, flies down from its perch onto the center of floor. Emannon sees the raven and gestures that it should leave.

"Begone, black scavenger!"

The raven then transforms itself back into Fontune. Emannon at first reacts with surprise, then stares at him with distrust. Fontune smiles as he approaches her.

"You've learned much while I've slept," says Fontune.

"My teacher was great," she says coldly, cruelly, "and my time...well spent."

Emannon's monkey jumps from the table and attacks Fontune. But as it lunges for Fontune's throat, he swiftly hits it with the back of his hand and knocks the monkey against the wall. The monkey screeches out in pain as it smashes its head. It hobbles away and sulks in a corner as it licks its wounds.

Fontune grabs Emannon's hand and holds it as she tries to pull away. He twists her wrist and looks into her scarred palm.

"A sad disfigurement," says Fontune.

"Not so," answers Emannon in cold hate, "'tis but the seal of a pact that I made with myself."

Fontune tries to take her into his arms, but she pushes him away. Once more he starts at her, but with the flick of her hand she causes a vase to leap off a shelf and hurl itself at him. Fontune quickly causes the vase to explode in midair: it shatters and its pieces fall to the floor.

Emannon and Fontune circle about each other. She shoots a bolt of energy at him, which he quickly deflects. Next she shoots out two, then three bolts in quick succession, all of which Fontune is able to duck or deflect. With his own flow of energy he forces her against the wall and starts to slowly remove her clothing. She struggles against his energy, but Fontune takes her into his arms, pulls her head back by her hair, and kisses her lips.

To get revenge, while he's kissing her Emannon transforms herself into an ugly old toothless hag with decaying flesh. She mockingly laughs at him as he pushes her away with disgust and revulsion. In anger he strikes her with a bolt of energy that makes her scream out in pain and forces her to transform back into her natural form. Fontune intensifies the energy until she finally submits from the pain.

"Enough, Fontune, enough," moans Emannon.

He then takes her into his arms and pulls her down to the couch.

Hours have past. Fontune continues to sleep on the couch as Emannon stands over him. From a nearby table she picks up a dagger and pulls it out of its sheath. She holds the knife to Fontune's neck. As he sleeps, each breath brings his neck closer and closer to the knife.

"So simple...so easy would it be for me to right these wrongs. One quick movement and justice would be done." She continues to stare at Fontune as she holds the knife at his neck.

"But wait," she says to herself, "no longer a lover, but just a piece of living flesh that will be my tool, and only a fool destroys her tools before her work is done. The Elixir... once you've gotten me that, then you'll sleep forever."

She takes the knife away from his throat, and stares at the remnants of the gargoyles that lie scattered about on the floor.

"There must be better ways...more effective techniques. For such skills...perhaps I'd be willing to make a trade." She then leaves the room.

Emannon stands in front of the mirror in her bedroom, as she vainly admires her beauty. A cool breeze blows through the room as the drapes flow and billow. Emannon wraps her arms around herself in order to keep warm from the chill. She turns to see Monde standing near her bed.

"The chill announced your presence."

136

"A way to instill in you a need for warmth," answers Monde.

"Much time has passed since your last visit."

"Did you think I'd forgotten you?"

"Perhaps your interest was brief," she answers coyly, "and passed quickly."

"Not so, but in these regions the price of ice is cheap."

"Yes, but even the frigid frost thaws with time."

Monde approaches her but Emannon steps away from him.

"With your strength you can take my body, but come, let us barter for my love."

"Much can I teach you," answers Monde.

"And I'm in need of many tricks," retorts Emannon, as she lightly touches his arm. "A pleasure for a secret."

"A fair bargain," answers Monde.

"Then I pray, sir, that you may come often."

Monde takes her into his arms as Emannon runs her fingers through his hair. They embrace and kiss.

31

Michael walks alone through the forest where he first met the elf and fairies. Suddenly fairies begin to flutter around him, and the elf appears from beneath a bush.

"Did you get it?" asks the elf.

"What?" asks Michael.

"The emerald, man, the emerald."

"I had it in my hands," Michael says sadly, "but it was stolen from me."

The elf becomes angry. "Then you've failed, and nothing is what you'll get from me." He starts to walk away from Michael.

"Wait! I lost the emerald, but in its place gained this." Michael holds his palm out above the ground. From the earth he able to draw some of the green energy which flows into his hand. The fairies become excited and flutter about.

"The healing power, it's back, it's back," they cry out. "Get Fudollda! Quickly, bring Fudollda."

Several of the fairies quickly whisk away. Within moments they return. Between them they carry a small fairy child with a broken wing.

"Heal Fudollda, so that she can fly again. Heal Fudollda," they all plea.

Michael takes the fairy child from them and holds it within his left hand. She's beautiful but also extremely fragile. One of her wings is broken and hangs limp as the other lightly flutters in the breeze. She looks up at Michael with her eyes filled with hope. With his right hand Michael draws more of the power from the earth. He then places this hand over the child and then covers her with the green flowing energy. Slowly her wing begins to mend until finally it is back to normal.

Fudollda stands up and cautiously flaps her wing. She then flaps it more forcefully and lifts herself up from Michael's hand. The other fairies flutter about gleefully. Michael sits on the ground and happily watches Fudollda and the others fly above him.

"Thank you, Michael, thank you," cry out the fairies.

Then, in unison, they all produce a white powdery substance which they sprinkle over Michael. As the powder falls on him, the forest around him begins to change. The colors and shapes transform as Michael enters another dimension. He does not become unconscious, but instead keeps his eyes wide open as he watches the magnificent alterations occurring around him. Objects begin to take shape and materialize, as colors and sounds stabilize, and Michael finds himself in a new world where everything he perceives seems to be slightly distorted. Angles are slightly out of whack, colors are a bit too brilliant, and there appears to be a transparency to everything around him.

Dwarf-like creatures, the Solwoes, move about near him. They, too, appear to be slightly distorted. They are not so grotesque as to be abhorrent, but nearly so. The Solwoes gather around Michael. He stands and tries to walk, but with great difficulty. His knees wobble. He has problems with his sense of balance and is overwhelmed by the distortions. The Solwoes speak among themselves in voices that have a tinny and reverberative effect, but what they say is unintelligible to Michael.

Another group of Solwoes approaches him from the distance. Within their midst is a small hooded figure, about three feet high. It's dressed in monk-like clothing, with a large hood on its head that completely covers its face. The small figure stands about ten feet in front of Michael, with a Solwoe on either side. They hold on to the creature's arms in order to help support it. They then slowly begin to lift up the creature's hood in order to reveal its face. The sounds of the atmosphere become almost overbearingly loud as the visual surroundings become more and more distorted.

Michael covers his ears with his hands and his eyes with his arms, as he cries out in pain. He cannot yet look at the face. The Solwoes stop lifting the hood and slowly lower it without revealing the figure's face. They then gently lead him away. The intensity of the sounds and the visual distortions subside as the other Solwoes begin to depart. The colors and images stabilize as Michael leaves this dimension and returns back to the woods by the babbling brook. Fairies flutter about as Michael hangs his head in shame.

"Did you see him?" ask the fairies. "Did you see his face?"

Michael sadly shakes his head in denial.

"Then journey on, journey on," they call out.

"But to where?" asks Michael.

"Towards the sun," they reply.

32

Suzanne stands over the kitchen sink as she scrubs dirty pots and dishes. The cook carries in more pots and lays them down on the counter.

"When you're done with these, there's more to be cleaned."

Suzanne is exhausted. Sweat pours from her face.

"I need to eat."

"When you're done, my pretty, when you're done. And I suppose you'll be wanting a place to stay for the night."

"Yes, if that can be arranged."

The cook laughs. "Anything can be arranged, but it'll cost you the floors."

Suzanne looks at the filthy floors with disgust.

"The world's filled with hungry beggars," says the cook. "I owe you nothing. Do the work, if you want the bed. Otherwise, be gone, and good riddance to you."

The cook walks out, leaving Suzanne tearful about her desperate state.

142

33

Michael walks through a deserted canyon. The walls of the canyon are lined with caves. Eyes peer out at him from the darkness of the caverns. Michael sees the glowing eyes but not the faces. He walks through a passageway and into a clearing. There, among the rocks, Michael sees figures standing about. They are covered with white sheets and wrapped in decaying bandages. Some, who are missing limbs, hobble on crutches. Close to Michael's right is a figure with bandages on its head. The figure turns towards Michael. It is a human face, but it has no nose. The nose has rotted away. Michael suddenly realizes that he is in a leper colony. He recoils in horror from the face, then runs towards the center of the clearing. The lepers walk towards him. The cripples move slowly as they beg for help. Michael feels trapped. He is afraid of these people: afraid of coming in contact with them and catching their dread disease. He cowers away as they continue to encircle him.

Then, from within their midst, comes the cries of a baby. A leper couple, a man and a woman, approach Michael. They carry a child in their arms. They hold it up in the air and out to Michael. It's a perfectly formed human baby, with no deformities. Michael is humbled. He takes the child and looks into its face. The child is beautiful. The child stops crying as

Michael holds it. The leper couple turn and walk away, leaving the child with Michael. The crowd disperses. After a few moments, Michael walks out of the leper colony with the child in his arms.

34

Suzanne is finishing her meal at the kitchen table. She is dirty, exhausted, and very unhappy. On the floor near her feet is a bucket filled with dirty water. She picks it up and carries it to a sink where she dumps the water. Glancing out through the open door she sees the cook talking to the two ruffians. Suzanne silently tiptoes closer to the door so that she can overhear their conversation.

"She's a pretty lass and will fetch you some fine coin," says the cook.

"Aye, she will at that, and some pleasure too, I suspect."

"Be that as it may, all I ask is but a small finder's fee, then you can do what you will," replies the cook.

The two ruffians grin at each other, then take out a bag of coins. They hand two gold coins to the cook. She angrily shakes her head, grabs the sack, and takes out another five gold coins. The men protest as she throws the sack back at them.

"The Turks will pay plenty for her fair skin and yellow hair," says the cook.

"Cold-hearted whore," they reply.

"Hey, she's no kin to me. She'll be in the loft above the barn. Take her after midnight."

The cook then gets up from the table and heads back towards the kitchen. Suzanne quickly goes back to the sink. She starts to fill up the water bucket as the cook re-enters the room. The cook surveys Suzanne's work on the floor as she drops the gold coins into her purse.

"Not bad," says the cook. "Wash it over once more and you've earned yourself a room for the night, in the loft above the barn. Finish here, then up to bed."

The cook leaves the kitchen. Suzanne quickly takes off her apron and runs out the back door.

Suzanne runs through the forest, away from the lights of the inn. She doesn't stop until she can no longer see the lights. By this time she is far into the forest, near a small stream. She sits down against a tree trunk, wraps her shawl around her shoulders, and tries to fall asleep.

35

At the foot of a mountain, near a village, Michael stands with two matronly women and a group of small children. He hands them the child. They take it and head back towards the village with the other children as Michael continues to journey up the mountain.

It is midday as Michael reaches the top of the mountain. In the sky above him blazes the golden sun against a cloudless deep blue sky. Michael readies himself by relaxing his body and staring down at the cool green grass. He then slowly lifts his head up from the ground until he is staring into the sun. He keeps his eyes open for a few moments, then closes, them. In the darkness behind his eyelids he sees a pink spot: the afterimage of the sun. Michael then turns his head towards the ground, opens his eyes, and looks at the cool green grass. He then again shuts his eyes and the blackness is filled with the color pink. Michael recalls an image of the leper colony, and in his mind covers them with this pink vapor.

After a few moments the pink color disappears. Then Michael once again slowly lifts up his eyes until he is again staring into the sun. The rays of the sun blaze the sky. This time Michael keeps his eyes open for twice as long as before. He then shuts his eyelids and once again the blackness is filled with the color pink.

Again Michael lowers his eyes to the ground and looks into the grass. When he closes his eyes he forms an image of the European continent, which he then covers with pink vapors. Next he forms an image of the revolving earth, and this he envelops within the pink hues. After a few moments the colors and images subside into the blackness. Michael reopens his eyes.

In the distance, at the foot of the mountain, Michael sees a male and female child playing. He looks at nature about him: the mountains to the north, barren plains to the east, green valleys to the south and forests to the west. Then, for the third time, Michael looks into the sun.

The sun blazes above him, but this time he holds his eyes open for much longer than before. Finally, after what seems like an eternity, he closes his eyelids. But this time, instead of seeing the color pink, the after-image is that of a brilliant green cross, a cross that radiates a green light that illuminates the darkness.

Michael blinks his eyes for a second, sees the sun, then shuts them again. Now, merged with the image of the green cross, is a green circle.

The green cross radiates within the center of the circle, then slowly the cross slides down through until it forms the sign of woman.

The horizontal bar on the sign of woman then drops down and forms the sign for man.

The symbol breaks apart until there exist side-by-side

148

Elixir

the sign for man and the sign for woman.

After a few moments the symbols merge back together and form a new sign.

The female crossbar then moves down and the sign becomes the double male symbol.

The double male symbol then moves up and becomes a double female symbol.

The double crossbars then separate from the rest of the symbol, leaving a circle with a line coming out of its bottom.

Then the circle and the line separate. This leaves an image of the three green signs against a black background: the circle, the equal sign, and the straight line.

The circle unravels and forms a straight line of equal length to the other line.

Both lines then curve into circles of equal size and form the image of a circle, an equal sign, and another circle.

They merge into a circle with a verticle line running down through the middle and the equal sign in the center of the circle and the verticle line.

This symbol then slowly rotates about its axis until it finally stops, with the straight line in a horizontal position, as the symbol for Elixir.

Michael reopens his eyes and looks about him.

149

"Then they're equal," he softly says to himself. "Madimi, Madimi," he quietly calls out.

A mist appears on the side of the mountain and then out of this mist comes Madimi riding on a unicorn. Madimi is having a hard time holding on as the unicorn runs at a gallop. She holds onto its mane for dear life with one hand as she tries to keep her flower laurels on her head with the other hand. Finally the unicorn comes to an abrupt stop as it tosses its head down and flings Madimi off its back. She lands on her rump with a thump. Her clothes are all disheveled. She gets up, rubs her sore rear end and takes a swipe at the unicorn with her wand. She misses as the unicorn quickly backs off. She takes her anger out on Michael.

"Now what do you want?" she asks.

"I've solved the riddle."

"Well, it's about time. It took you long enough. What have you got?"

"They're equal."

Madimi is unimpressed as she rubs her sore rear. "You know, sometimes you humans are really much more trouble than you're worth. Is that it?"

Michael becomes less confident. "A new symbol."

"Well, let's see it," demands Madimi impatiently.

In the air before them Michael produces the image of the circle, the equal sign, and the straight line. He then

150

merges the three together to form the new sign.

"Well," says Madimi, "that should hold you for another millennium or so."

Madimi then attempts to get back on the unicorn. But the unicorn bolts and Madimi again falls to the ground. She gets up and begins to chase the unicorn who is slowly galloping away.

"The god of love, Madimi. You said I had to solve the riddle first," yells out Michael.

"And you have. That symbol is the key, not me," she says as she continues to run after the unicorn. Then, to herself, she says, "These people are going to have to learn how to take care of themselves."

Michael watches Madimi disappear into the mist after the unicorn. He pauses for a moment in order to reflect on what he should do. He then whispers the name "Suzanne," and produces the new symbol in the air in front of him. Michael concentrates, and transmits all the energy that he has onto the symbol, which intensifies in illumination as it absorbs the energy. It then produces the humming sound of the realm of the Solwoes. Light from the symbol begins to transforms the colors and shapes around Michael as he enters the dimension of the Solwoes.

Again he finds himself in the same distorted atmosphere as before, and once again he is approached by the Solwoes with the small hooded figure in their midst. Michael stands before them, ready to look at the creature's face. The Solwoes slowly begin to lift up the creature's hood. Again the intensity of the distortions increase. Michael remains calm and relaxes his body as he continues to look at the creature. Finally the hood is removed to reveal the ugliest creature in the universe, with a grotesquely disfigured face consisting of distorted layers of flesh. Michael trembles, feels sick, yet tries to remain as calm and relaxed as possible.

"Kiss the god of love," say the Solwoes. "Become a friend and kiss the god of love."

Michael reaches out for the god's hand, which is like that of a deformed child. Michael kisses the hand, as the god sighs heavily.

"No, not the hands," say the Solwoes, "but the face. Kiss the face of love."

Michael then approaches the god and softly kisses the face. The Solwoes then put the hood back on its head as they lead their child god away from Michael. One of the Solwoes remains behind.

"Humans cannot stay long in this dimension, for if they do, their minds and bodies will be destroyed."

"Suzanne?" asks Michael.

"It will be taken care of," replies the Solwoe.

Together they watch the god of love being led away. The Solwoe speaks to Michael. "Born of a human mother who died in childbirth. Deformed, rejected by

152

all others, lives as ruler of the land where all abandoned children go. Now can you understand why it would never show it's face to man? Only a creature who has known the pain of complete rejection could ever generate enough love to fill the universe."

"What is his name?" asks Michael.

"He...she... is called Compassion," says the Solwoe, as he turns and walks away from Michael. The intensity of the sounds and distortions begins to subside as the environment quickly transforms back to the mountaintop. Michael then lies down and sleeps.

36

It is night as Kelly, Dee and Jane sit about a campfire. Poohfer is sound asleep in the wagon as the cat, with vengeance in its eyes, sits and watches him from another part of the wagon. Kelly is rubbing the crystal ball in an effort to make it work. After a few moments he gives up out of frustration.

"I'm sorry, John, but it seems to have lost its power," says Kelly.

"Try again," says Jane, "for it just may be a question of faith."

Though Jane has said this innocently, both men eye her with suspicion.

"I've got to know the formula for the Elixir," says Dee. "My whole life's work can't end like this, not when I'm so close to the answer." Dee is in torment as he tries to make a decision. Finally, he says, "I've got to know! Then so be it." He turns to Kelly. "Okay, Edward, tell Madimi that I agree and try that crystal again."

"Agree to what, John?" asks Jane.

Kelly whispers to himself, then rubs the ball. Suddenly, in a puff of white smoke, Madimi appears in the air above them. This time she is riding on a beautiful white swan. Madimi gleefully laughs as the swan flies to and fro through the air. Madimi winks at Kelly and then, with a wave of the wan, sprinkles stardust over the three of them.

Jane begins to giggle as Dee grins from ear to ear. Dee laughs boisterously. Kelly is beyond himself with glee as he sits on the log like a babbling idiot. Dee slaps Kelly on the back out of friendliness and almost knocks him into the fire. Jane laughs so hard that she falls backwards off of the log. She lands on her back with her legs sticking up in the air as her petticoats fall down to her waist. Both Dee and Kelly look at her and laugh.

They all roll about the ground. Madimi flutters up into the air until she's about ten feet above them. From this vantage point she looks around to make sure no one else is in the vicinity. She spots Poohfer in the carriage. With the wave of her wand she quickly puts him into a deeper sleep. His limbs respond by becoming completely relaxed.

Dee and Kelly each grab one of Jane's legs and pull themselves up alongside her body until the lie on either side of her. Both men begin to kiss her. Madimi then sprinkles more stardust over the three of them as they gleefully laugh.

Back in the wagon, as Poohfer snores away, the cat walks up along his body and proceeds to sit on his face.

37

Suzanne sleeps in the forest next to the stream. From the distance a little wagon drawn by a donkey approaches her. Driving the wagon is the Solwoe who last spoke to Michael. He is dressed in human clothes and could pass for being an ugly little dwarf. Suzanne awakens from the noise.

"Hello there," calls out the Solwoe.

Suzanne gets up. Her clothes are in tatters and she is very dirty. The Solwoe gets down from the wagon and begins to start a campfire.

"Are you hungry?" asks the Solwoe. "Would you like to share my breakfast?"

"At what price?" asks Suzanne suspiciously.

The Solwoe sadly looks at her. "I think you've been alone too long. No price."

Suzanne laughs at him. "We'll see."

The Solwoe looks at her torn clothing. "Why don't you bath in the stream. I have extra clothes in my wagon that you can have."

Suzanne snickers. "Now, we're getting to it, huh."

"And what do you have to fear from me?" he asks as

he gets the clothes from the back of the wagon.

"Why should you give me something for nothing? No one else does," she says. "If there is one thing that I've learned, it's that there is no one I can trust."

"Why don't we imagine that I'm doing a favor for someone who loves you," he says. "There must be at least one such creature in the world."

Suzanne clutches onto the amulet still hanging about her neck.

"Bathe while I prepare some breakfast," he says, "for I cannot stay here that long."

Suzanne takes the towel and clean dress from him and walks towards the stream.

***

Suzanne finishes her breakfast as the Solwoe prepares to leave. He goes to the wagon and after a few moments returns with a white dove in a bird cage. He presents the caged bird to Suzanne.

"One more gift before I go," he says.

Suzanne is overwhelmed by his kindness. "But why?"

"While many in the world are cruel and selfish, not all are so. Remember that, Suzanne, and that it's best to stay among those who love you."

He then boards the wagon.

"When you're ready, express your heart's desire to

the dove, then let the bird fly free."

With that the Solwoe drives away into the forest. Suzanne watches him until he disappears among the trees and mist. After a few moments she opens the cage and takes the dove into her hands.

"Go and fetch the man who loves me."

She tosses the bird up into the air. It flutters its wings, then flies away into the distance.

38

Dee, Jane and Kelly are still asleep on the ground. It is now morning. Kelly sleeps contentedly with his arms around Jane's feet while Dee sleeps with his head on her breasts. All their faces show smiles of contentment. Madimi sits on the ground just a few feet away from them. She hums to herself as she happily makes a laurel out of some flowers. Her swan, which is tied to a small tree with a ribbon, sits on the ground beside her.

Suddenly Madimi looks up from her work with concern when she hears a loud humming sound. The swan begins to flap its wings. Madimi then notices a shimmering light beginning to materialize. With concern she looks over at the three naked people lying on the grass.

"Uh, oh!" she says to herself.

She quickly mumbles an incantation. Then, with the wave of her wand, she quickly tries to redress the people. But the spell doesn't work correctly and she gets their clothing confused. She puts Jane's dress on Dee, Dee's clothes on Kelly, and Kelly's clothes on Jane. Madimi stomps her foot in frustration as Samuel begins to materialize.

Madimi levitates up from the ground and floats

towards Samuel. She attempts to block his view of the threesome as she tries to perform the correct wand movements behind her back. Again the clothes become rearranged, but this time they are even more mixed up than before. Each person wears part male and part female clothing.

"What are you up to now?" asks Samuel. He sees the threesome and becomes aghast as Madimi wrinkles her nose up at him.

"Dee needed this," she flippantly replies. "No harm done."

Samuel takes Madimi by the arm, turns her over his knee, and spanks her. She cries out with pain and indignation. Her screams awaken the threesome. They all have intense headaches.

"This definitely won't do, Madimi," says Samuel. "Now go do some good," he says as he slaps her once more on the rear, before he puts her down.

Madimi begrudgingly departs as she rubs her sore fanny. She unties the ribbon leash from the tree and drags the swan away with her, as Samuel dematerializes.

Dee rubs his eyes as he tries to wake up. He then sees Kelly put his hand on Jane's knees. Dee becomes concerned, then angry as he starts to remember the previous night. Kelly and Jane become worried as they watch the change of expressions come over Dee's face.

"Now, John," says Kelly, as he senses trouble brewing.

Jane begins to cry as she sees Dee slowly starting to lose control over his emotions. Quickly he goes from jealousy to rage as he stands up and starts towards Kelly. Dee is wearing Jane's dress, and Kelly has on her petticoats. Dee loses his balance as he trips on the dress and falls to the ground. Kelly runs away.

"POOOHHFER!!!" yells Dee.

Poohfer is still sleeping in the wagon with the cat sitting on his face. He begins to stir at Dee's call, but has difficulty breathing. Poohfer struggles to pull the cat off him, but the cat in turn digs its claws into Poohfer's face. He screams out in pain.

Dee then gets back up and runs after Kelly as Jane covers her face with her hands and cries.

39

Michael is still sleeping on the mountaintop as the white dove flies through the air and settles down next to his ear. The dove begins to coo. This awakens Michael. He stretches out his limbs, yawns, and sits up. The dove continues to coo. Michael puts out his hand and the dove jumps into it. Michael then stands up with dove in hand.

"Where to, little bird?"

The dove flutters up into the air and flies a bit above Michael's head.

"I wish I too had wings so that I could fly and find my love."

Michael then has a thought. He looks at his arms and legs, considers them pensively, then quickly begins to spin himself around. As he does this he transforms himself into an eagle. The eagle spreads wide its wings, then takes flight with the dove.

The eagle and dove fly in the air over the countryside. In the far distance below them stands Suzanne next to the stream. The dove continues to fly down to Suzanne, as the eagle turns away and lands in a nearby clump of bushes. The eagle then transforms back into Michael. As he approaches Suzanne, she sees him and runs to him. They embrace and kiss.

"How did you find me?" asks Suzanne.

"The dove showed me the way."

"Oh, the dove. It was gift from the dwarf."

"A dwarf?" asks Michael.

"Yes, a strange fellow..." Suzanne pauses, then takes hold of the amulet that she still wears about her neck. "Michael, I know who you are."

He looks at her with concern. "And if I weren't a wizard's son?"

"But you are, and that's all that matters, for we're together again and all our dreams have come true."

He still has some concern, but is happy to back with her. "So tell me, what have you learned on the road?" he asks.

"That it's better to be with friends and people that love you." She then takes hold of his arm as they walk towards the stream. "And that companionship brings happiness. And you?" she asks Michael.

He ponders for a moment as he stares at their reflections in the stream. Finally Michael speaks as he smiles at her. "It's compassion that leads to love."

40

Prague, Bohemia. Dee, still depressed about the previous day's events, drives his wagon through the streets of Prague. Jane still sobs as she sits next to him. Kelly dejectedly sits in the back of the wagon next to Poohfer, whose face is all bandaged up because of the cat's scratches. The cat triumphantly sits across from Poohfer. She licks her paws with pride as she watches him.

The streets are filled with people going about their daily business. Dee stops the wagon and calls out to a man passing by.

"Please, sir, which way to the street of the alchemists?"

"There, around to the corner," says the man as he points the way.

Dee continues to drive until they reach the corner. He then stops the wagon, hops down, and ties the reins to a railing. Kelly and Jane get down from the wagon. Poohfer slowly starts to get up.

"Stay with the wagon," Dee says to Poohfer, "and watch the belongings."

Poohfer quietly sits back down without making a comment. Dee starts to leave, but he senses that something is wrong and turns back to Poohfer.

"Are you all right, Poohfer?"

Poohfer doesn't utter a word, but instead just sadly stares at Dee. Dee then shrugs his shoulders and walks away.

Dee, Jane and Kelly walk down a street filled with medieval vendors who are selling their wares from the booths set up along the sidewalk. The market is filled with colorful blankets, clothes, jewelry, crockery and alchemical/astrological paraphernalia. Grobel, Emannon's servant, leans against a building as he watches the crowd in the market. He notices Dee and party because of their different style of dress and begins to follow them.

Suddenly, from opposite sides of the street, two alchemists run out from their respective shops. Each has a vial of liquid in his hand. One is an old man in his seventies, the other, a younger man in his thirties. They are both overcome with excitement.

"I've found it! The Elixir!" shouts the old man.

"The Elixir! I've found it!" yells the young man at the same time.

They stare at each other with mutual disdain and distrust as a crowd gathers around them. Dee and party move closer to watch the scene, as does Grobel. The young alchemist thrusts his vial out at the older man.

"The Elixir!!! I discovered it first," he says, then mumbling under his breath, he adds, "you old creep."

The older alchemist likewise responds in a whisper. "Young punk." Then to the crowd he proclaims his triumph. "The Elixir!!! 'Tis my discovery."

Grobel steps forward from the crowd. "A test! Let's have a test!!" The crowd agrees and roars its approval. "A test, a test. Here now, a test! The old man first."

The young man arrogantly faces the crowd. He snarls and bares his teeth at them. "No!!! I was here first!"

The crowd respond in unison. "The old man first, the old man first!"

The young alchemist growls at them, but finally gives in and with resentment steps back. The old alchemist snickers at him, then walks into the center of the street. The crowd backs away and gives him plenty of room. He lifts up the vial, stares at it with hope and expectation, then quickly gulps it down. The young alchemist looks on with envy as the crowd roars with approval.

The old alchemist proudly smiles with great satisfaction, as the young alchemist hangs his head in disappointment. Then suddenly the old man begins to shake violently. His hair falls out of his head, his teeth fall from his mouth, and he becomes stiff as a board. He then fall down to the ground, dead. The crowd sighs with sympathy.

"AAAHHHHHHHHHHH......"

They then all turn and stare at the young alchemist,

for now it is his turn. He fearfully looks at the old man, then at the waiting crowd, and finally back at the vial in his hand. He gulps as the crowd continues to watch him with expectation.

Suddenly the young alchemist becomes very animated as he tries to offer the vial to members of the crowd.

"Elixir of life?" he offers, "Panacea to cure all ills?"

A grin of fear is frozen upon his face as he tries to please the crowd, but the crowd in turn boos him and starts to disperse.

"BOO!! BOO!! FAKE!! PHONEY!!"

He continues to offer the vial to members of the crowd. People walk over the body of the dead alchemist as they leave.

Then, in the midst of all this turmoil, Kelly walks forward and holds up the sack of red powder. "Wait, wait!!" he shouts.

Dee tries to pull him back but it's too late. The crowd turns and considers the newcomer.

"I may not have the Elixir," says Kelly, "but here in this sack are pieces of the philosopher's stone."

Grobel looks at Kelly with great interest. "Can you turn base metal into gold?" asks Grobel.

"That I can, and I'll put it to the test for any man."

The crowd responds favorably. "A test, a test!"

But Grobel, mean and ugly, quickly spins around and glares at the crowd. "Enough tests for today. This one will be done in private, for the Baroness. Now disperse!"

The crowd grumbles with disappointment as it disperses. Dee whispers into Kelly's ear.

"Careful, Edward, for once the powder's used up, it cannot be replaced."

"He said a Baroness, did you hear that? Before royalty, Dee. Finally, royalty."

Grobel stands in front of Kelly and looks him over from head to toe.

"How is it that one who has the ability to turn lead into gold dresses like a beggar?"

Kelly is at first embarrassed, but then recovers nicely.

"We've traveled for many days," he says with slight indignation. "You don't expect me to wear my finest clothes while on the road, do you?"

Grobel bows with respect to Kelly. "Then it's settled. The Baroness will expect you at eight."

After Grobel leaves Kelly becomes filled with excitement. He turns to Dee and Jane. "Tonight, with royalty!" He then looks down at his clothes. "But first, a shop for new clothes."

"And what about us?" asks Jane.

"Oh, no need," he says hurriedly. "I'll just present you as my servants." Kelly then excitedly runs down the street.

41

Emannon and Fontune stand on her balcony as Grobel kneels before them.

"He said he can make gold?" asks Emannon.

"That he did, and that he possessed pieces of the philosopher's stone," replies Grobel.

"Why waste you time with such people?" asks Fontune.

Grobel looks at him as if he were crazy. "What? Gold, man, I'm talking about gold!"

"The attraction of fools," answers Fontune.

"But they may also possess the key to the Elixir," adds Emannon.

"Very unlikely, for those who seek gold would never be able to recognize the purer substance. You waste your time. Only the emerald, together with the amulet, can show us the Elixir," says Fontune.

Emannon goes to her chair. From beneath it she pulls out a small chest. With greed in his eyes, Grobel watches her every move. She opens the chest and takes out a gold coin. She then places the chest back beneath her chair. She holds the coin out to Grobel. "Here, Grobel."

He quickly scurries over to her and takes the coin. Suddenly there is a loud knocking on the castle doors. "That must be them," says Grobel.

"Then show them in," replies Emannon.

Grobel quickly leaves.

"Let's see what they have to offer," says Emannon. "We've nothing to lose, and your impatience has resulted in worse before."

"If I'm impatient it's due to my need to be free," says Fontune.

Emannon laughs. "Is it freedom that made you serve Monde so faithfully?

"You misjudge me, Emannon, I'm not an evil man."

"I've known worse," she replies. "You're just filled with a selfish need for power.

"Not selfish, Emannon, for the Elixir is rightfully mine, and unjustly denied by my father."

"So you served his enemy instead."

"So that one day I need serve no one. My father made peace with Monde. I seek to rid the earth of him. The tricks he teaches will one day be used to bring about our liberty."

"That, or provide him with amusement," she answers. "Perhaps the Elixir is not to be given by the stars that rule your destiny."

Now, more like my old father do you sound, he that sought to live beneath the laws of nature. Should I, because of a day, a week, a year...let the Elixir slip through my hands? No, cursed be the name of man if I dare not reach out and grasp that which I desire...if I settle for less than I know I deserve. Have I not hands? Then I will use them. Have I not a mind? Then with thoughts I will weave my schemes. And with this voice I will not cry out in protest, but instead softly, sweetly, entice my desires into my arms. I shall not acquiesce to the will of cold indifferent spheres that plot to make me less than I know I can be. I shall be controlled by no other, and my dreams will be realized, or I will cease to be." Fontune places his hands on her shoulders, but Emannon steps away from him. He's saddened by her rejection.

"I know that in my haste...I abandoned you, and in the heat of desire...treated you roughly," he says. "For these things I ask forgiveness, and hope that in time we can start anew."

Emannon becomes pensive as she steps away from Fontune. Deep in thought, she rubs her hands together. She glances down at her scarred palm.

Fontune continues. "For when I've won, you'll be my queen."

Emannon hears this, then softly whispers to herself, "Ah, but have I need for a king?"

42

Grobel opens the massive front doors of the castle. Outside stand Dee, Kelly, Jane and Poohfer. Jane carries the cat in her arms. Kelly is dressed in a new suit of clothes. They are ill-fitting and don't become him in the least.

"Come in, come in," says Grobel.

The party walks through the door. Grobel closes it behind them and bolts it shut. They all look at him with suspicion.

"Just a precaution," says Grobel, "to keep the riffraff out."

Kelly smiles in agreement. "Yes, that makes good sense."

The party follows Grobel down the hallway. Kelly has difficulty walking in his stylized shoes and tight clothing.

Emannon is still looking away from Fontune as Grobel enters the room, followed by the guests. Grobel presents Kelly to Emannon.

"Ah, the famed alchemist who can turn lead into gold," she says.

Kelly bows before her. "Edward Kelly, madame, your

173

humble servant."

"And these?" asks Emannon as she points to the other people with Kelly.

Kelly downplays their importance. "But my servants who help with the experiments."

"To be quite frank, Mr. Kelly, the rumors of your abilities have excited me. Would you mind giving us a demonstration?"

"Why, not at all."

"Then this way, please."

She leads them to a furnace at the far side of the room. Along the wall stand six clay gargoyles, who are now inanimate. The cat meows in fear when she sees them.

"How would you like to be dinner for that, you over-grown rat," says Poohfer. The cat hisses at him and he quickly protects his face with hands.

"Fearsome creatures," says Kelly.

Emannon lovingly moves her hands over one of the gargoyles. "My little creations," she says tenderly.

The furnace already has a hot fire burning within it. Grobel places a piece of lead into the pot, then the pot into the furnace. Kelly takes out his sack and starts to carefully tap some red powder into the pot. But Grobel accidentally knocks into his arm, and causes Kelly to dump all of the powder into the pot. Kelly quickly clutches his chest to forestall a fatal cardiac arrest.
174

"OOOOHHHHHHH!!!!" he cries out in agony.

"Sorry," says Grobel, as he walks to the other side of the furnace.

Tears come to Kelly's eyes as he watches the solution dissolve. Everyone gathers closer to the furnace as they watch the lead begin to melt. Then, to their satisfaction, the lead transforms to gold before their very eyes. Grobel greedily takes the pot from the flames and pours the liquid gold into a mold.

Emannon is happy with the demonstration.

"Very impressive, Mr. Kelly. May I see more of this substance?" asks Emannon.

"Unfortunately, our supply is depleted," he says as he turns the empty sack upside down.

"But of course you have the knowledge to replenish it," she replies.

Dee coughs. Kelly looks to him for help, but Dee just turns away.

"Well, actually..." starts Kelly, "...to be perfectly honest with you, I found that."

Emannon smiles at him. "Come, come, Mr. Kelly, don't try to be shrewd. One does not find pieces of the philosopher's stone. You must make more. I insist."

"Madame, I must confess. I do not have that ability."

"But we have laboratories here, and methods to enhance one's memory."

Fontune steps forward. "Enough of this. Have you knowledge of the Elixir?"

"The Elixir, sir?" asks Dee.

"Yes," answers Fontune as he studies Dee.

Dee lowers his eyes and feigns ignorance. "Only of what they say in the streets."

"I think that with the passage of time and the intensity of hunger, their tongues will loosen."

Kelly is shocked by this response. "Madame, this behavior is quite unbecoming of royalty."

"Not at all," she replies.

Kelly becomes confused. "Well, then it's at least highly inhospitable."

"Ah yes," she says, "that is true." Then to Grobel, "Lock Kelly in the tower alone and the others in the laboratory, until they decide to cooperate."

Dee steps forward. "Madame, I object. I will not tolerate this behavior."

"Nor I," asserts Poohfer.

The cat meows and hisses at Emannon. Poohfer looks at the cat with respect. "That's right, fierce feline." The cat meows a thank you to Poohfer in acceptance of his recognition of her.

Kelly steps forward. "Madame, as you can see, we are united in our resolve that any attempted incarceration will not be tolerated."

Emannon becomes angry and utters an incantation.

Grobel speaks to Kelly. "Whoa, boy, now you've done it. Went and got her mad, you did."

"So?" replies Kelly with great confidence.

With a wave of her hand Emannon then activates the six gargoyles. They are armed, and menacingly approach Dee and party.

"Either go now peacefully, or later, in pieces, be carried out," says Emannon.

"The former of the two options would be preferable," says Kelly as he bows to Emannon. Dee quickly kicks him in the rear.

Kelly turns to Dee as they are being lead out by Grobel and two of the gargoyles. "I told her the truth," says Kelly. "See what good honesty gets you around here."

After they have all left the room Fontune approaches Emannon.

"As I said, you waste your time with the likes of these. Only the amulet can help us now."

"This amulet, can you produce an image of it?"

"Yes, of course," answers Fontune.

"Then come here."

Together they walk to a cauldron. Its bubbling fluid produces a mist which hangs in the air above its surface. Emannon waves her hand over the cauldron as she utters an incantation. The cauldron boils faster as the mist grows thicker. Emannon points into the cauldron.

"In there, produce an image of this amulet."

Fontune concentrates, and within the mist appears an image of the amulet. Emannon then utters another incantation. They watch as the mist around the amulet transforms. It becomes the face of Suzanne with the amulet on a chain around her neck. The image then changes into a full body view of Suzanne. She stands alone near a tree with a mountain in the background.

"I know that peak," says Emannon. She calls out to her gargoyles. They walk to the cauldron and peer at the image of Suzanne.

She cackles with glee as the four gargoyles fly off the balcony into the open sky. Yet she is unaware of Fontune's fascination and admiration of Suzanne's beauty.

43

Suzanne and Michael are sitting together on the grass.

"Show me some magic," Suzanne asks.

Michael hesitates. "These powers are new to me."

"Do anything," she replies.

Michael concentrates, and in the air in front of them produces the new symbol.

"I like it, but what is it?"

"A new symbol, for us," answers Michael.

"Show me some more."

"I don't know any tricks."

Suzanne fiddles with the amulet about her neck. "Are you sure that you just didn't find this amulet?"

Suzanne starts to jump up, but Michael grabs hold of her and pulls her back to the ground.

"And what magic can you do?" he asks.

"Have your children," she replies.

"But not without me to share in that task..."

"...that pleasure," she says as she interrupts him. She then pushes him off her and runs away. Michael rolls over onto his back and laughs. "Best not run too far. The forest is filled with wolves, you know."

Suddenly Suzanne screams. Michael turns to see her being picked up by the gargoyles. He runs to help her, but it's too late. All he can do is watch as they fly away with her.

After a few moments, Samuel appears. Michael runs towards him.

"Father, help me. They've taken Suzanne."

"She'll be safe for the time being. But the Elixir, Michael, is of more importance now, and it is that which they want."

"Who?"

"Fontune and Emannon, and it's them you'll now have to fight."

"This Fontune, do you know him?"

"Yes," says Samuel, "for he's your brother, and my first-born son."

44

The gargoyles carry Suzanne onto Emannon's balcony. They lay her down on the floor. Suzanne looks up and sees Fontune. Since he's an extremely handsome man, she is naturally attracted to him. Fontune smiles down at her with interest in his eyes. Emannon becomes jealous as she notices the attraction between them. Suddenly Suzanne snaps out of the daze and defiantly stands up.

"What is this?" she demands.

Emannon walks to Suzanne and quickly slaps her, knocking her back down to the ground. She then grabs the front of Suzanne's dress and tears the amulet from her neck. Suzanne glares at her with anger, and starts to get back up. But the gargoyles approach her with drawn swords, and she decides that it's best to sit back down.

Emannon gives the amulet to Fontune. He takes the emerald from his pocket and places it in the center of the amulet. It makes a perfect fit. He then holds them up in the air and utters an incantation. A ray of sunlight hits the object. This, in turn, produces an image of the Elixir in its crystalline vial in the space before them. But it is only an image, and not the real thing. When Fontune reaches out to grasp the Elixir, his hand passes through it. Emannon laughs.

"Yes, it does show the Elixir, doesn't it?" she says in a mocking tone.

Fontune feels humiliated. In his anger he pulls Suzanne up from the floor.

"The Elixir, give it here!" he yells at her.

"I can't," she says. "I don't have any magical powers."

"Then how did you get this?"

"It was a gift?"

"It was gift."

"From whom?"

Suzanne shakes her head and refuses to speak. "No, I won't betray him."

Fontune laughs. "There are ways. Think of him."

With a wave of his hands Fontune directs a flow of energy at Suzanne, which freezes her into standing position. He then tries to draw out an image of Michael from her forehead. Suzanne struggles and cries out in pain, but it's of no use. Fontune continues until he has extracted the image of Michael from her. The image floats lifelike in the center of the room.

"The boy that awoke me! Why of course, it must be he who has the Elixir."

"To the cauldron," shouts Emannon.

Fontune moves the image across the floor and places it within the cauldron's mist. Emannon utters an incantation, and within moments an image is seen of Michael at the edge of the forest. Emannon laughs.

"He's but a young man. I'll handle this," she says.

"How so?" asks Fontune, "For it's she he loves, not you."

Emannon stares at Suzanne, who is lying unconscious on the floor. "Then it's her I'll become," Emannon replies, as she slowly transforms herself into an exact replica of Suzanne. Emannon laughs, then vanishes from the room.

45

Poohfer, Dee and Jane sit on the floor of the laboratory in a state of hopelessness and depression. The cat sits on Jane's lap. Finally Dee speaks.

"Well, I guess we might as well start working. Poohfer, get the furnace going."

Poohfer doesn't move. Dee looks at him with surprise.

"Poohfer, did you hear me?"

"I heard you, John. If I can hear you in my sleep, I surely can hear you when you're five feet away."

Dee becomes impatient. "We don't have the time for..."

"John, it seems that time's all we do have here," Poohfer responds with quiet resolve.

"What's wrong, Poohfer?" asks Jane.

"John's wrong, or better yet, it's me that's been wronged," he answers. "Oh, I don't mind that in all the years that I've worked for you, you never once invited me home for supper. But that's all right, for I understand the difference between an employee and a friend. And I guess I really don't mind you ordering me about. When you pay a man's wages, you're entitled to those liberties. But neither one of us will be exchanging coin in this cell, John."

"We'll not be here forever, Poohfer," says Dee softly.

"Maybe, maybe not," he replies. "But the name's not Poohfer, John, it's Paul. Poohfer was your joke of a nickname."

"If I wronged thee," says Dee with concern, "it was an oversight. My work fills my mind. I can't think about..."

"Trivial things," answers Poohfer. "But that's not the real problem, John. In all the years that I worked for you, not once did you say, 'Good work, Poohfer. Well done!" Tears start to brim up in his eyes. "Not once, 'Good job, Poohfer, well done!'"

They all sit silently. Then, after a moment, the cat gets up from Jane's lap and walks to Poohfer. She rubs herself against the side of his leg, then climbs onto his lap. Inadvertently, Poohfer starts to pet her.

46

Suzanne still lies unconscious on the floor as Fontune stands above her and stares at her with desire in his eyes. He bends down on one knee and takes her into his arms. Her breasts heave as she breathes deeply. Fontune lays her head on his knee as he tenderly caresses her face with his fingertips. He then slowly bends towards her and kisses her lips. Suzanne slowly regains consciousness as she putts her arms around him and becomes engrossed in the kiss.

Suddenly, she opens her eyes, realizes she's with Fontune, and struggles against him, but his grip is too strong and she cannot break free. Finally, she scratches the side of his face with her fingernails. He yells out in pain as he drops her to the floor. Fontune puts his hand to his face, then looks at his fingers and sees blood. He becomes angry.

"Why fight me, when your eyes and body show your true desire."

"That's not true, for I love another."

Fontune laughs and mocks her. "A mere boy."

"Not so, but a great wizard, " she says proudly.

"I think not."

"But it's been prophesied."

"By whom?"

"An old gypsy woman. I'm to marry a great wizard, the true owner of the amulet."

"Then gaze upon your husband, wife, for this is rightfully mine. It was my father's, and I'm his first-born son. By the laws of men this belongs to me."

Suzanne becomes confused. "No, that's not possible."

"But it's true," answers Fontune, "and here you are bringing the amulet back to me. So the prophecy is about to be realized."

"I don't believe you. What about this witch?"

"Emannon? She's grown cold and indifferent with the years," he says sadly. "Perhaps it's best that I let her pass."

"And to me you'd vow forever?"

Fontune admires her youth and beauty. "But of course."

Suzanne is now really confused as to what she should believe.

"But be patient," says Fontune, "for this day will resolve all questions, and you have but to wait for night."

47

Michael stands at the edge of the forest as he looks at Emannon's castle in the far distance. Suddenly Emannon, disguised to look like Suzanne, appears about twenty feet away. Michael is overjoyed to see her. He runs to her and they embrace.

"Are you all right?" he asks.

"Yes, yes, I'm fine."

"What did they want?"

"The amulet."

"My father's amulet? But why?"

"They hoped it would bring them the Elixir. But when that failed, they no longer needed me, so I was set free."

Michael holds her closely in his arms. "I'm so relieved that you're safe and with me again."

"The Elixir, Michael, can you produce it?" she asks coyly.

"I don't know."

"I've always wanted to see it, to touch it. Would you try? For me, please?"

"For you, Suzanne?" He then kisses her lightly on the lips. "Yes, of course I'll try for you."

Michael relaxes his body as he begins to concentrate. A beam of light grows at his forehead. He focuses the beam on a spot in space in front of them.

"Elixir," he whispers, "Elixir, reveal yourself to me."

As Michael intensifies the beam, the spot transforms and emits the colors of the rainbow. This continues until finally the Elixir appears. Emannon's eyes open wide with excitement, then she quickly reaches out to grab the Elixir. But as her fingers are about to touch it, a flash of electrical energy bolts out from the Elixir and strikes her hand. Emannon screams out in pain. The shock transforms her out of Suzanne's form and into her normal shape. Michael steps away in surprise. The Elixir quickly transforms back into its rainbow hues, then vanishes. Michael approaches Emannon.

"Who are you and what have you done with Suzanne?"

Emannon, in pain and rage, lashes out at him. "Damn your Suzanne, and your Elixir, too."

She then quickly disappears. Michael starts to walk into the vast plain that lies before the castle.

48

Kelly paces his cell. He peers out through the barred windows to the ground below. He is at least thirty feet above the ground. In anger and frustration he pulls at the bars. Some of the cement at their base gives way from age. A glimmer of hope flashes in his eyes. He quickly tiptoes to the door and looks out into the hallway. Not seeing anyone, he runs back to the windows and tugs on the bars.

His tight-fitting clothes make all his movements awkward. He has difficulty pulling the bars loose. He grabs one of the bars with both hands and places his feet against the wall. He then pushes against the wall with his feet as he pulls on the bar with his hands. Finally the bar comes off as Kelly falls down to the floor on his back. He clutches the bar to his chest as a manic grin of desperate hope spreads across his face.

He jumps up, again looks at the distance to the ground, then falls down to his knees and prays.

"Oh Lord...I've been a wicked, wicked man, and I'm ashamed to even beg for your consideration. But if you help me Lord...oh Lord...if only you'll help me now in my time of desperation, I swear to you I'll end my evil ways." He smiles up to the sky with feigned hope in his heart.

"I've seen the light, oh Lord, I'll be good, I'll be honest, I'll be reverent, I'll..."

"Work hard," says a deep, profound, unseen voice.

The smile of an easy salvation slowly droops from Kelly's face as he utters a deep, regretful sigh.

Then, with resignation, he says, "Oh Lord...show me the way out of this mess...and I'll obey all thy Tenets."

Kelly then slowly stands up. As he looks about the room he sees the bed and gets an idea. He quickly runs to it and tears off the sheets.

49

Fontune stands on the balcony overlooking the plains below, as Suzanne watches him from behind a column. She is still perplexed as to what she should do, for when she looks at Fontune she's uncertain as to whether or not she's really looking at the man of her dreams.

Suddenly Emannon reappears in the middle of the room. She paces about the room in a rage.

"So you also failed," says Fontune.

"I touched it, had it within my grasp, but it sparked and burned. Now revenge will be mine. Go, kill the boy!" she orders the gargoyles.

The gargoyles snarl and growl as they head towards the balcony. Fontune grabs Emannon's arm.

"Call them off," he says. "That method was tried years ago and proved disastrous. I'll not wait another twenty years."

Emannon pulls away. She's angry, but knows he's right. The gargoyles hesitate as they wait upon her command.

"Back," she commands them, "for your time has not come yet."

The gargoyles retreat from the balcony. Emannon then notices the scratches on Fontune's face. She smiles with contempt as she glares at both Fontune and Suzanne.

"I see you've been faithful to me once again," she says to Fontune. He touches the side of his face, then with embarrassment begins to speak.

"We..."

"Don't bother. The Elixir is all that is important, but this time you'd better have good help." Emannon closes her eyes and softly whispers, "Monde."

In a dark corner of the room Monde begins to materialize. When in full form he approaches Emannon, smiles, touches her elbow with his hand, then stands beside her as he watches Fontune. Fontune suddenly understands their relationship. He is deeply hurt, yet bears it well, as Emannon cruelly smiles at him. Suzanne watches the three of them from behind a column.

"Your time has come. Use well what I've taught you, and soon you'll be ruler of all the land."

Fontune slowly, but with feigned respect, bows down on one knee before Monde. "In my absence, you've taught her well. Once I possess the Elixir, I'll be sure to repay you," Fontune says softly, insidiously.

"This time I'll be near," adds Monde.

Fontune stands up and looks at Emannon.

"Give me your blessing," he asks.

"What? You need the help of a woman?" she answers with quiet contempt. Fontune lowers his eyes in defeat, then graciously bows to her before he turns and leaves the room.

50

Dee and Poohfer are still sitting against the wall of the laboratory, as Jane paces about the room. Finally, she sighs deeply and speaks.

"I can't cry anymore, John. What's done is done."

"Ah, so much for remorse," answers Dee.

Jane becomes angry. "What happened you brought upon yourself, John Dee, and I'll no longer feel guilty about it. But we must do something, otherwise we'll wilt like that hay in the corner."

It is getting hot. Dee takes off his jacket and lays it on the floor next to him. Suddenly Jane gets an idea. She looks at Dee's jacket, then back to the straw. She picks up his jacket and goes to the pile of hay.

"Poohfer, come here," says Jane.

Poohfer, who is still petting the cat, looks up at her but doesn't move.

"Please, Poohfer, I need your help."

He gently puts down the cat and goes to Jane.

"Here, stuff his jacket with hay," she says.

Poohfer becomes uncomfortable. "Well, I don't know.

I think he's had enough for one day."

"Poohfer! Please do as I say!"

As Poohfer begins to stuff the jacket with hay, Jane goes to the cell door and peers out. At the far corner of the hallway sits Grobel. He's stuffing himself with food. Jane looks away, shakes her head with disgust, then turns to Dee.

"John, I've always had faith in you, and been devoted to you, but now it's time for you to trust me."

Jane begins to rearrange her clothes in order to become more sexually attractive. Poohfer stops his work as a leer spreads over his face. Dee becomes embarrassed.

"Jane, I'm changing my ways," says Dee, "but do you think that here, in front of..."

"Oh quiet, John," she says.

Back in the tower, Kelly has finally finished making a rope out of the sheets. He ties an end to the one remaining bar, then throws the rope sheet out the window. Its length is only a third of the way to the ground, which is much too short. He quickly looks around his cell, but there is nothing else that he can use. Then he glances at his new clothes. After a moment, he regretfully sighs, then quickly begins to undress.

51

Monde puts his arm on Emannon's shoulder, but she steps away.

"There will be enough time for that later, but first I think you should be with Fontune."

"As you wish," says Monde, as he slowly dematerializes. Suzanne steps out from behind the column. Emannon approaches her. On the table before them lies the amulet and emerald.

"Did Fontune promise that you'd be his new bride?" Emannon then points to the gargoyles. "Before the evening's done, they'll be the lovers in you wedding bed."

"How easily you two manage your betrayals."

"Tell me," says Emannon, "what powers do you seek? Nature has already given you beauty that makes slaves and fools out of men, weak creatures that they be. Walk into any room and watch then grovel for your attention. What, would you rather draw a sword and chance that your own blood be spilt, while instead you could stand back, watch, and let the victor be your slave?"

Emannon picks up her dagger from the table. She feels its fine edge as she moves it across her palm. She then hides it among her garments. She caresses one of her gargoyles.

"Fontune is now no more to me than one of these clay creatures. I need no man," says Emannon.

"And what of love?" asks Suzanne.

"Undulations of the emotions caused by the phases of the moon. Best to be discharged and done with."

"You know, it's people like you who give witches a bad name," responds Suzanne.

A sneer freezes on Emannon's face.

"And you? Is Fontune your choice for happiness?"

"No, I think not, for betrayal, once practiced, becomes a habit. I'll take Michael, whatever the outcome of the battle may be."

"Then come," says Emannon, "and watch your lover die. Take her," she orders the gargoyles.

Two gargoyles grab Suzanne and lead her to the balcony.

52

Grobel is sitting at the table stuffing himself with food when he hears a voice call out his name.

"Grobel!!!!"

Grobel looks up and sees Jane's hand sticking out through the bars. She's waving a white handkerchief. He eyes it suspiciously as he walks to the cell door.

Grobel peers through the bars, as Jane stands next to the opening and smiles at him. Back by the furnace stands Poohfer who partially blocks Grobel's view of the stuffed strawman wearing Dee's jacket. Dee stands against the wall by the door, out of Grobel's line of vision. He holds a thick log in his hand. Jane lowers the dress on her shoulder in order to be more seductive. Grobel smiles, rubs his hands, then stares at her lustfully. Jane winks at him, as he wipes his greasy mouth with his sleeve.

"What about the old man?"

"He's so busy with his work he'll never miss me."

Grobel then snickers as he opens the door. When he walks into the room Dee knocks him out with the log. Dee, Jane and Poohfer quickly tie him up and prop him up against a corner. Dee then puts his arm around Poohfer's shoulders and points to the chemicals on the counter.

"Poohfer, go doest what thou does best."

Poohfer smiles broadly and stands a bit taller as he walks to the work table. He then starts to slop together a bunch of chemicals. Dee goes to the straw dummy and starts to take back his jacket. Jane stops him.

"Leave it be, John. That's the old you. A new man deserves new clothes."

Dee smiles and kisses her as she throws her arms around him. Meanwhile, Poohfer looks around the room for more chemicals. He breaks open a closet door. Inside, the closet is filled with barrels marked "GUN POWDER." A manic grin spreads across his face.

With the chemicals that he had already mixed, he hurriedly makes a trail across the floor to the closet door. Then, at the far end of the trail he places a three-inch-high candle. Poohfer lights the candle, as Dee removes the keys from Grobel's belt.

"Quickly, we must find Kelly," says Dee.

The three of them run out with Poohfer shutting the door behind them. The cat then slowly walks out from under the table. It sits down in front of the closed door and meows, as the candle continues to burn at the end of the chemical trail.

In another part of the castle, Kelly stands completely naked in his cell as he ties the last bit of his clothing to the sheet rope. He then lowers the rope through the window. Dee, Jane and Poohfer quickly run down the hallway, looking into the various cells for Kelly. Poohfer walks past a cell just in time to see Kelly, completely naked, climb through the window. Poohfer waves to the others. Dee quickly opens the door with the keys he took from Grobel, and they all enter the cell.

Kelly has already started down the rope. Only his head still appears above the window when the others enter the cell. Kelly smiles and waves to them.

"Sorry guys," he says, "But every man for himself."

With that, the last metal bar breaks away from the window. Kelly screams as he falls, until he hits the ground with a sickening TTTHHHUUUMMMPPP. Then he emits one long moan. The others turn away from the window and shake their heads in disbelief.

53

Fontune stands at the base of the castle as he looks across the open fields. As he starts to walk forward, the spirit of Samuel appears before him.

"So, you've returned to watch the final fight," says Fontune, "one that need never have taken place if you fulfilled you obligations."

"And given the Elixir to you?"

"Yes, that simple."

"You, who would abuse it as you do the truth."

"Honesty is for children. Why should I be honest with those who would twist my words into lies that they'd use against me? Honesty for the honest, and lies for the treacherous."

"But can you tell the difference?"

"Perhaps, but what of the innocents who watch as you speak your lies. They don't know of your plans, and you'll lose their love and respect. Then having no one to believe in, they'll be won over by the deceivers who'll enslave them with pleasures as they point out your deceptions. What about the children?

"They will grow up to understand," answers Fontune.

"Unless it's too late," replies Samuel.

Fontune becomes angry. "If not I, who? And if not now, then when? The threat is not this boy, but Monde, as it always has been."

"This boy is Michael, my second son."

"Then in the second position he should stay. He doesn't understand Monde's treacheries. Only I do, and only I can beat him."

"Perhaps."

"I do understand him very well," reasserts Fontune.

"Yes, for under his tutelage, you've become like him."

"Give me your support, and let us end this fight."

"No, there's more at stake here than just my flesh and blood, for in the wrong hands the power of the Elixir will be used to enslave. There's nothing more to be done," says Samuel, and with that he disappears.

54

Dee, Jane and Poohfer run towards Kelly, who lies in agony at the base of the castle tower. They try to lift him but he moans out in pain. He indicates that both his arms and legs are broken.

"Quick, get some sticks," Dee says to Poohfer.

Poohfer gathers sticks for a cast. Jane removes some petticoats and tears them into strips of cloth for bandages. Suddenly Poohfer yells out and points towards the plains. "Look, out there!"

Dee stands up and puts his hands over his eyes to block out the glare of the midday sun. Jane also stands, as Kelly desperately tries to twist his head in order to see. He cries out in pain with every move he makes.

Emannon and Suzanne stand on the balcony overlooking the plains. Emannon turns to one of the gargoyles.

"Let's end this quickly. I can't kill him, but I can weaken him. Wound the boy."

One of the gargoyles picks up a bow and arrow, aims it, then lets the arrow fly.

55

On the plains in front of the castle, Michael and Fontune stand alone.

"So we meet again," says Fontune.

"But not as before," responds Michael.

Michael hears the sound of the arrow speeding towards him. He gracefully steps to one side and catches the arrow in his right hand. He then snaps it in two and drops it to the ground at Fontune's feet.

"The Elixir! Give it to me!" demands Fontune.

"No," says Michael.

"Then I will take it," replies Fontune.

Fontune lifts up his hand and directs a bolt of energy at Michael. It hits him in the chest and forces him back. Michael leans forward as he struggles against the energy, but it keeps pushing him backwards. He suddenly produces a mirror-like shield that deflects the energy beam from him onto a nearby rock. The rock begins to sizzle from the heat.

Fontune then directs two energy beams at Michael, but he's also able to deflect these. Fontune sends out a third beam, which Michael also blocks. Then

Michael quickly retaliates by sending out one of his own beams under the other three. This catches Fontune by surprise, hits him in the chest, and nearly knocks him over. The pain from the blow forces Fontune to lose the power to maintain his energy beams.

Fontune levitates a huge boulder which he then hurls at Michael, who, in turn, destroys it in midflight with a bolt of energy.

Fontune then laughs, and sneers, as he takes a step towards Michael. He opens wide his cape. Out scurry small demons and evil-looking spirits. They run across the field and pounce on Michael. He doesn't know how to fight them. He tries to back away, but they jump on top of him and knock him down to his knees. They kick him and pull at his hair. As they are about to overwhelm him, he looks up to the sky and sees the sun. He pulls together whatever strength he has left, and produces an image of two large metal doors. He stands up in front of these doors, then slowly opens them wide to reveal the burning fires of Hell.

The Demons cover their eyes and curse Michael as they back away. Fontune responds by producing a large dark cloud. Rain pours down from this cloud and extinguishes the flames. The demons once again start to advance forward, but when they are just a few feet away, Michael spreads wide his arms and produces an image of the blazing sun. The sun grows larger and larger in size as it engulfs the clouds and all the demons who are near it. The remaining demons quickly run away from Michael. Even Fontune backs away as he covers his eyes with his cloak to protect himself from the brightness.

Fontune then turns his back to Michael, looks eastward, and raises his arms up to the sky. The winds begin to howl as the sky gets darker. Clouds quickly speed by as hurricane winds blow. The demons quickly scurry out of the plains as they climb up the side of the mountains that line the valley.

A tremendous roar is heard from the east. On the horizon appears a gigantic tidal wave, at least fifty feet high. It roars across the plains towards Michael and his blazing sphere. Fontune laughs as he levitates up into the sky so as to hover above the crashing waves. Michael calmly relaxes as he watches the fifty-foot wall of water rush towards him. Then, when it is about a half-mile away, he also begins to levitate. But as he does a mountain grows up out of the earth beneath him. He rides on top of the mountain until it is a hundred feet above the onrushing water. The waves crash against the mountain's sides, but cannot destroy it. After a few moments, the water recedes and flows out of the valley. Michael and Fontune stare at each other. Michael is serious, but Fontune enjoys himself as he laughs and rubs his hands together in glee. He sneers at Michael as he utters another incantation. The earth begins to rumble as the mountain quakes beneath Michael's feet. He quickly flies away as the mountain's top is blown away by a volcanic eruption. It spews out hot lava and belches forth grey ash clouds that fill the horizon.

Michael then turns to the north, lifts his arms up to the sky, and produces a cold wind which blows away the dust cloud. The wind freezes the mountain top and stops the flow of lava.

Fontune next produces a blackness which completely covers the valley up in darkness. In response, Michael fills the blackness with stars. Once again the two men face each other across what looks like the blackness of space.

To his left Fontune produces the image of the moon revolving about the earth by gravitational force. Michael becomes pulled towards Fontune by this same force. He struggles, but the power is too great. Fontune is about to put his hands around Michael's throat, as Michael looks to the right. There he sees the earth within the gravitational pull of the sun, and locks himself into that force field. He quickly speeds away just as Fontune is about to grab him.

Fontune next produces a fiery comet which he hurls at Michael. As it approaches, Michael produces a black hole, whose magnetic power sucks up the comet and begins to drag Fontune into its center. Fontune is overpowered: he cannot escape and he cries out to Michael for help.

The darkness clears away and once again Michael and Fontune are on the plains in front of the castle. Fontune lies on the ground as Michael stands over him.

"So I retain the Elixir," says Michael.

"Not so fast, my young friend," says Fontune, as he lowers his face to the dust and whispers, "Monde, Monde."

The dust begins to swirl as it turns from brown to black. Then, from out of this blackness, appears Monde in his human form.

"So you are the stronger of the two," Monde says to Michael. "Join me and above the earth you will rule."

Fontune laughs. "Join him and he'll use you as his tool."

Monde lashes out at Fontune as he strikes him with an electrifying bolt of energy. Fontune screams out in pain.

"I'm not interested in ruling others," responds Michael.

"Very well, then simply relinquish the Elixir," Monde slyly answers.

Michael looks down at Fontune who is bent over with pain, then turns back to Monde.

"No, I think not."

"Think that you'll always be young, that your flesh won't feel the pain of disease and decay? That it, too, won't rot?" asks Monde, as he creates a mirror in front of Michael. As Monde continues to speak the mirror reflects the aging transformations of Michael as he gets old and decrepit.

"Immortality I cannot guarantee, but longevity and health, yes, if you worship and pay homage to me. I can forestall the inevitable, which is this."

The mirror shows Michael dead. His body rots, decays, and becomes the foodstuff for the worms and maggots that crawl out of it.

"Only I can forestall this," says Monde. "Serve me and I'll make your time on earth pleasurable, filled with sensual delights. Without me, view your destiny."

Michael stares into the mirror, but does not flinch from the sight.

"No Monde, you lie," says Michael, "for the spirit survives, the spirit survives."

"Illusions of the mind. Power is all that matters, for there is no soul that goes beyond the physical. There is no eternity, and I am man's only hope," responds Monde.

Michael steps back from the mirror, then speaks quietly. "You stop too soon Monde, for the process does not end here. The body will be interred, put back into the ultimate womb from whence it has sprung. Look into the mirror, Monde."

The mirror reflects the image of the decaying Michael as he is interred within the earth and covered with dirt. On top of this dirt grows green grass, then flowers. A young child walks past and picks up the flowers, laughs, then joins her parents as they walk off to have a picnic.

"Herein lies my true destiny, Monde. You can say that there is no eternity, but that is false, for the process itself is the eternity."

"And what of consciousness, will that a petal become?" asks Monde.

"If there be no consciousness, then also no pain, nor need for you."

"I offer you long life!!" shouts Monde.

"No, you offer me slow death, for you want finality, the end of the process of change and transformation through which life becomes revitalized, and in which we participate for all time. You hope for that dead, static, final state of things that somehow you think you can control and form into your own image. Yours is a goal based on the fear of participation, not the joy of life!"

"Silence," hisses Monde.

"It continues," says Michael.

"Silence, I said!" screams Monde.

Michael smashes the mirror into a thousand pieces of glass, in order to reveal a bright blue sky filled with white puffy clouds and sunshine.

The wrath of Monde grows dark and gloomy as he transforms himself into his large snake form and hisses at Michael. Michael backs away and leans against a rock as the snake opens wide its jaws as if to devour him. Michael stares into its large, hypnotic eyes. The sky grows to be dark as night. Then, from out of the snakes' eyes a thousand others appear and move around Michael in the darkness. Everything becomes distorted: sounds intensify as shapes collapse and converge. Among all this the laughter of Monde is heard. Michael is driven down to his knees. He looks up to the darkness and sees the leering grin of Monde's human face.

"Do your worst, Monde," says Michael, "for I have already looked upon the face of love."

With this, Monde transforms himself into a series of horrifying and terrifying images that descend upon and attack Michael. But still he looks on and doesn't flinch. The distortions intensify as all shapes and sounds collapse and converge. A cloak of black inky darkness weighs over Michael and weakens him further, until finally he calls out.

"Suzanne, Suzanne, give me what strength you have."

Suzanne and Emannon stand on the castle balcony as a storm wind howls and the plain below is filled with blackness. Suddenly she hears Michael's voice calling out to her.

"Suzanne, give me what strength you have!"

Suzanne drops down to her knees, bends her head towards the plains, and lets flow all the energy she can towards the spot where she last saw Michael.

As she does this, she prays, "Michael, I send you all my love." She then collapses to the floor of the balcony.

Within the darkness Michael sees a flash of light beam down towards him. It's just enough energy to help him form an image of the new symbol.

The sky lights up around the symbol and the distortions produced by Monde are filtered through with light and transformed into those of the land of the Solwoes. Monde is transfixed by the change. The grin disappears from his face as he struggles to break free from the forms that bind him. He becomes encased within this other dimension, and it solidifies and constrains his movements as he struggles to be freed. Monde transforms back into his natural form as the snake and completely solidifies. Finally the petrified snake form begins to crack and break apart until it crumbles into a pile of dust on the ground. As the other distortions in the air subside, a light gust of wind blows the dust remains of Monde away into the air as it spread them across the desolate plains.

Michael stands with dignity as Fontune still lies on the ground, cowering from Michael's might. Fontune then stands. He quickly transforms himself into the black raven and flies towards the castle. Michael watches him depart. He then transforms into an eagle, spreads wide his wings, and takes flight after the raven.

56

At the base of the castle tower, Poohfer and Dee are lifting Kelly into the wagon as Jane sits up in the front holding the reins. Kelly is in splinters with casts on both legs and one arm. They look up to the sky just in time to see the black raven land on the castle's balcony. The raven then transforms back into Fontune. Poohfer and Dee are amazed by this and in their shock drop Kelly into the back of the wagon. When he hits the wooden floor he moans out in pain. They then quickly hop into the wagon and start to drive away.

Back in the castle laboratory, the candle at the end of the chemical trail has burned three-quarters of the way down. In a window sill sits the cat. She meows as she looks out over the plains.

Dee and party are driving away when they see a large eagle fly by overhead. They watch as the eagle lands on the balcony and then transforms into Michael.

"It's Michael," shouts Dee. "I must warn him about the explosion."

Dee jumps off the wagon and starts to run back towards the castle. Suddenly, Jane realizes that the cat is missing.

"The cat? Where's the cat?"

Everyone looks about for the cat. Suddenly they hear a lone meow coming from the distance. They look and see the cat sitting in the lab window, high above the ground. Then they all slowly turn and look at Poohfer.

"Ah hell, I'll save the cat," says Poohfer. He and Dee run towards the castle.

57

Michael walks in from the balcony and is confronted by Emannon and Fontune, with Suzanne between them. Fontune holds a knife to Suzanne's throat. As Michael steps towards them the gargoyles, with bows and arrows drawn, move out from the shadows.

"Stay where you are," orders Fontune, "for this knife and those arrows are not the stuff of illusions."

Michael stops.

"A simple trade, brother," says Fontune. "A life for the Elixir."

"I'm not your brother," answers Michael.

"But you are, for we both sprang from the same thrusts into our mother's womb."

"Perhaps brother in flesh, but definitely not in spirit. But for peace's sake, I'll be willing to share with you what I can," says Michael.

Fontune considers this. Emannon sees that he is wavering, and quickly whispers in his ear.

"No need for that. Take it all, it's ours. With Monde gone, we'd be supreme."

"The Elixir," says Fontune, "give it over."

"No," says Michael.

"Is it worth her sacrifice, brother? Then see the color of your true love's blood."

Fontune pricks Suzanne's neck with the knife and draws some blood. Michael starts towards him, but then the gargoyles pull back the bow strings. Again Michael stops.

"Let her go," says Michael.

"The Elixir," answers Emannon.

With resignation, Michael lifts up his arms.

"Elixir, come to me," he says sadly.

The air in front of Michael transforms as the Elixir appears in its crystalline vessel. Michael reverently reaches out and takes it into his hands. He then walks towards Fontune, who approaches him with Suzanne. They meet in the center of the room. Emannon goes to Fontune's side. Michael holds out one hand to Suzanne. She takes his hand. He then holds out the Elixir to Fontune, who takes it as he releases Suzanne. Suzanne and Michael embrace as they back away. Both Fontune and Emannon gaze with admiration at the Elixir.

"Seize them!" Emannon orders the gargoyles.

Two of the gargoyles quickly seize Michael and Suzanne and tie them to a column.

"Why?" asks Michael. "You now have the Elixir."

"So there's no longer any need for you, as there never was in the first place. And soon enough you'll return to that nature you love so dearly, but first, witness my final triumph."

Emannon leans against Fontune's shoulder as she places one hand into the folds of her garments.

"Our final triumph," she says.

Michael sadly turns to Suzanne. "I'm sorry, I never thought it would end this way."

She holds onto his hand through the ropes. "No, Michael," she whispers," there's always hope. The Elixir..."

Fontune lifts the vial up as he gazes at the Elixir.

"Now there will be no others before me," says Fontune.

Fontune drinks of the Elixir as Emannon eagerly waits at his side. When he takes the vial away from his lips, she grabs his hand and stares into his face with cold resolve.

Fontune holds the Elixir out to Emannon. She cautiously reaches for it, but this time there is no shock. She quickly drinks from the Elixir. When finished, she places the vessel on the table, tightens her grip around the dagger, and stares into Fontune's eyes as her lips curl with a smile.

Fontune slowly begins to glow with a blue-silver light as a golden hue begins to emanate from Emannon's body. The power flowing through Fontune intensifies as Emannon's body continues to take on a golden tone.

Fontune points his hand towards a stone column and discharges a thunderbolt of energy. The force hits the column and breaks apart pieces of stone. Fontune laughs with pleasure as he next destroys a stone vase. His laughter becomes manic as the power flowing through him intensifies. But the blue-white energy continues to grow and grow until it overwhelms him and he begins to disintegrate. He screams in anguish as he begins to melt until finally he is nothing more than a pool of evaporating liquid on the floor.

While this is happening, Emannon's golden tone becomes harsher as it starts to solidify. Her cold smile becomes frozen on her lips as she transforms into a solid gold statue, as exquisitely beautiful as any classic Greek sculpture.

As Emannon becomes petrified, the energy sustaining the gargoyles drains out of them and they revert back to their inanimate clay form.

Dee runs into the room. He quickly unties Michael and Suzanne.

"We must hurry," says Dee. "The castle's about to explode!"

They all start to leave, but Dee stops in front of the statue of Emannon and admires it.

"What exquisite beauty," says Dee, before he turns and runs out with the others.

58

Poohfer slams open the door to the laboratory and runs into the room just as Grobel finishes untying himself. Poohfer rushes to the window and grabs the cat. Grobel lunges at him but misses as Poohfer races for the door. The candle burns down and ignites the chemical trail. Grobel follows him out as the fuse burns towards the closet door.

Poohfer runs into Dee, Michael and Suzanne at the end of the hallway.

"Quick, run," says Poohfer, "the fuse is lit."

Grobel comes out into the hallway.

"Emannon will never let you escape," shouts Grobel.

"Emannon's dead," yells back Dee.

Grobel stops dead in his tracks. "Dead? Then who'll have her gold?" Grobel turns and runs back towards Emannon's chambers as the others run in the opposite direction.

Grobel runs into the chambers. He cautiously eyes the petrified gargoyles, then proceeds to the statue of Emannon. He admires it, then bends down to get the chest of gold coins under her chair. He pulls out the chest, opens it, and runs his fingers through the gold.

His face is filled with greed.

Suddenly a tremendous explosion shakes the room. Stone columns start to fall over and the ceiling collapses. A second explosion splits the floor in half. The gold statue of Emannon totters, then falls toward Grobel. He looks up and screams as the statue crushes him to death.

Richard Michaels Stefanik

59

Outside, Dee, Michael, Suzanne and Poohfer, with the cat in his arms, run away from the castle as several explosions rip it apart. When they reach the wagon, they all turn and watch the explosions. Dee puts his arm around Poohfer.

"Well done, Poohfer."

Poohfer proudly smiles as he watches the castle collapse. After the destruction has ended, Poohfer gets into the back of the wagon with the cat. Dee starts to climb up in front next to Jane, but he looks back and sees Michael and Suzanne are not getting aboard.

"Aren't you coming along?" asks Dee.

"No, there's another place we have to go," says Michael. Dee goes to Michael and hugs him. "Then I wish you both well." He hugs Suzanne. Dee climbs onto the wagon. There still lies a stack of books on the seat between him and Jane. Dee picks up the books and throws them out of the wagon. Jane then slides closer to him as she takes hold of his arm. They all wave goodbye, as Dee drives the wagon away.

60

Back in London, Dee drives the wagon up to the front of his laboratory. Dee and Jane get down from the wagon. He unlocks the door, and Jane starts to go in.

"Will you be wanting to work, John?" asks Jane.

"No, I'll be coming right up," he answers.

Jane smiles, kisses him on the cheek, then goes inside. Poohfer gets out of the wagon and approaches Dee.

"I'll not be coming in, John," he says proudly. "I've been able to save some coin and think it's time to strike out on my own."

Dee is disappointed. "You're always welcome here."

"Thank you, but I think this best."

Poohfer proudly holds out his hand. Dee takes it and they shake.

"You're a good man, Poo...Paul," says Dee.

"Yes, I know," answers Poohfer. Poohfer turns and starts to walk away. The cat sits by the doorstep and watches them. The cat looks up at Dee who then nods his approval. The cat meows and starts after Poohfer. Poohfer looks at the cat, then Dee. Dee shrugs.

Poohfer talks to the cat. "But if you come you'll have to carry your own weight, and be respectful." The cat meows in agreement. "Well, then, up with you."

As Poohfer reaches down, the cat jumps up into the palm of his hand and walks up his arm to his shoulder. He then lies on Poohfer's shoulder as they walk down the street.

Kelly slides out of the back of the wagon and hobbles towards the door on his crutches. Dee blocks his entrance.

"Sorry, Edward, but there should be but one man to a house. You'll have to be on your way."

"John, ye be harsh to a man of ill health," replies Kelly.

"Yes, that's true. Good day, Edward Kelly."

Dee then enters the lab and bolts the door shut behind him, leaving Kelly out in the street by himself. When Kelly turns to leave, he bumps into the body of the constable. Ann stands next to him. She is pregnant.

"Edward Kelly?" bellows the constable.

"Yes, that's him, Father," Ann goes to Kelly and takes him by the arm. "I'm sure he'll make a good husband, if but given the chance."

The constable slaps the nightstick against his palm.

"A decent, law-abiding, hard-working husband," adds the constable. They each grab one of Kelly's arms and drag him away. At first Kelly appears sad, but when he glances over Ann's plentiful body, a smile grows on his face. He shrugs his shoulders. Ann, slightly overcome with excitement, lightly tugs on Kelly's hair and bends two of his fingers.

"Ouch, that hurts," says Kelly.

"Sorry, dear, just got a little carried away."

Kelly smiles at her. "A charming habit, I'm sure."

"HA!!!" laughs the constable, as the three of them walk down the street.

61

Michael and Suzanne stand on a mountaintop, at the place where Michael was born. Below them lies the valley with one tall oak tree and the scarred remains of the burnt hut. Suzanne embroiders a piece of white cloth as she and Michael start down the mountainside.

They approach a small pond in the clearing before the tree. As they stand together, their images reflect in the water with the full sun to their backs. Finally, they walk towards the oak tree. As they come close, the spirit of Samuel appears among its branches.

"Welcome home, son."

"But I've lost the Elixir, and have returned empty-handed," says Michael.

"Empty-handed?" replies Samuel. "No, for as long as you have hope, the Elixir will always exist."

The spirit then holds out his hands and another vial of the Elixir appears. Samuel slowly vanishes as the Elixir sparkles and glitters. The crystalline glitter spreads among the tree branches, then down its trunk, until the whole tree shimmers. After a few moments the tree changes back to its natural color. Michael and Suzanne sit down at the base of the tree, as she finishes embroidering the cloth.

"There, now it's done," says Suzanne. She hands the

cloth to Michael. It's his new symbol for humanity, stitched in green thread against a white background.

"I like it," says Michael. He holds up the cloth so that the line through the center of the circle is vertical. Suzanne sighs deeply as she takes the cloth from him.

"No, not like that," she says, as she rearranges the cloth so that the straight line is horizontal. She places it down on the ground in front of them.

"It's like this."

Suddenly, the God of Love appears, accompanied by two Solwoes. The hood still covers her face. The Solwoes slowly lift it and reveal the face of Madimi!

"Madimi," cries Michael. "But why the disguise?"

"Kissing a pretty face is never a test of compassion. Only a test of appreciation...and good eyesight."

The Solwoes transform into Cherubs. Madimi sits in the branches of the tree and sprinkles rose petals down on them. Michael and Suzanne laugh as they playfully keep moving the symbol around, first with the line vertical, then with it horizontal, as Madimi sits above them, the tree behind them, and in the sky, to the left over Michael, the moon, and to the right over Suzanne, the sun.

"Oh, here we go again," says Madimi. "La dee da, la dee da."

Elixir

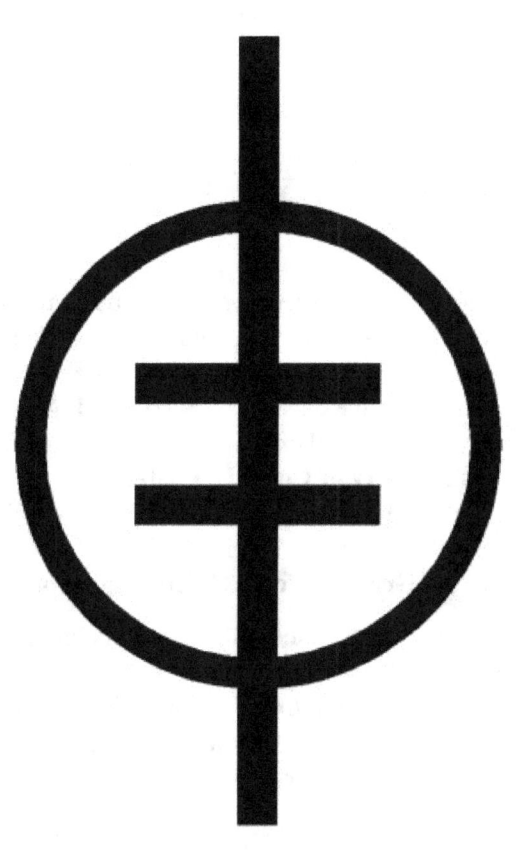

Richard Michaels Stefanik

Richard consults with new writers to develop original stories into high concept screenplays. He was a Fellow at the **American Film Institute** then worked at several Hollywood studios, including **Paramount Pictures** and **Walt Disney**. Richard has taught **Screenwriting** and **Story Design Seminars** in cities throughout the world, including London, Copenhagen, Orlando, Los Angeles, San Francisco, Las Vegas, New York, and Hollywood.

Richard taught a twelve-week story design workshop at **UCLA Extension**, and he has conducted classes at the **Creative Screenwriting Expos**. He has taught online classes for **Scr(i)pt Magazine**. In 2003 he lectured on comedy in London to the **British Society of Comedy Writers**. A French translation of **The Megahit Movies** was published by Editions Dixit in Paris in 2003, as **"Les Clés Des Plus Grands Succès Cinématographiques"**.

Richard has conducted a story design class in **New York** at the **Scr(i)pt Magazine PitchXchange**. He also lectured at the **Sherwood Oaks Meetings with Producers and Development Executives** at **Fox**, **Sony**, **Universal** and **Paramount** studios.

The Megahit Movies Hollywood Story Design Workshop™ has been held in **Orlando, Florida, San Francisco** and **Hollywood.** He now conducts his workshops at the **Hollywood Roosevelt Hotel.** In May 2006 he was a featured speaker in England at the **Oxford International Festival of Films.**

Richard Michaels Stefanik
THE MEGAHIT MOVIES
www.TheMegahitMovies.com

* TITANIC *
* STAR WARS * SHREK 2 * E.T. *
* THE PHANTOM MENACE *
PIRATES OF THE CARIBBEAN:DEAD MAN'S CHEST
SPIDER-MAN * REVENGE OF THE SITH * RETURN
OF THE KING * SPIDER-MAN 2 * THE PASSION OF
THE CHRIST * JURASSIC PARK * THE TWO TOW-
ERS * FINDING NEMO FORREST GUMP * LION
KING * HARRY POTTER: THE SORCERER'S STONE
* FELLOWSHIP OF THE RING * ATTACK OF THE
CLONES * RETURN OF JEDI * INDEPENDENCE DAY
* THE SIXTH SENSE * EMPIRE STRIKES BACK *
PIRATES OF THE CARIBBEAN * HOME ALONE *
THE MATRIX RELOADED SHREK * CHAMBER
OF SECRETS* MEET THE FOCKERS * THE
INCREDIBLES * THE GRINCH JAWS *
* MONSTERS, INC. BATMAN * MEN IN BLACK *

This website analyzes the Megahit Movies, those films which have generated more than $250 million in North American Box Office receipts. It presents principles of story development that can be used to develop popular movies by providing an analysis of cinematic techniques. The website is designed for writers, directors and producers who want to create commercially successful films. The fundamentals of dramatic structure, the human emotions, and the creation of humorous characters and situations are explained, with examples from the most popular Hollywood movies ever produced.

Richard Michaels Stefanik
www.TheMegahitMovies.com
rms@TheMegahitMovies.com

www.ingramcontent.com/pod-product-compliance
Lightning Source LLC
Chambersburg PA
CBHW071902220626
47052CB00002B/174